D0410315

Will wanted her. That knowledge gave Meg power.

Hell, she was an adult. There were no stars in her eyes any more; Graeme had doused those. Will had told her he had no plans to marry, no plans for a long-term relationship. Even if he'd changed his mind he wouldn't choose her. She couldn't give him a child, and he'd want a family. He loved kids.

But this wasn't happy families; she knew that.

This was reality. This was unmistakable lust.

She had needs like the next woman. She'd just survived a plane crash. Life was fickle and unreliable. She wanted him, and now she was certain he wanted her. And, damn it, this time she was taking what she wanted—even if it was only for a day and a night.

Always an avid reader, **Fiona Lowe** decided to combine her love of romance with her interest in all things medical, so writing Medical Romance™ was an obvious choice! She lives in a seaside town in southern Australia, where she juggles writing, reading, working and raising two gorgeous sons, with the support of her own real-life hero!

You can visit Fiona's website at www.fionalowe.com

Recent titles by the same author:

THE NURSE'S LONGED-FOR FAMILY
PREGNANT ON ARRIVAL

HER
MIRACLE BABY

BY
FIONA LOWE

MILLS & BOON®

All the characters in this book have no existence outside
the imagination of the author, and have no relation
whatsoever to anyone bearing the same name or names.
They are not even distantly inspired by any individual
known or unknown to the author, and all the incidents
are pure invention.

All Rights Reserved including the right of reproduction
in whole or in part in any form. This edition is published
by arrangement with Harlequin Enterprises II BV/S.à.r.l.
The text of this publication or any part thereof may
not be reproduced or transmitted in any form or by
any means, electronic or mechanical, including
photocopying, recording, storage in an information
retrieval system, or otherwise, without the written
permission of the publisher.

MILLS & BOON and MILLS & BOON with the
Rose Device are registered trademarks of the publisher.

First published in Great Britain 2006
Large Print edition 2007
Harlequin Mills & Boon Limited,
Eton House, 18-24 Paradise Road,
Richmond, Surrey TW9 1SR

© Fiona Lowe 2006

ISBN-13: 978 0 263 19539 2
ISBN-10:   0 263 19539 2

Set in Times Roman 15¾ on 18¾ pt.
17-0507-51534

Printed and bound in Great Britain
by Antony Rowe Ltd, Chippenham, Wiltshire

HER
MIRACLE BABY

Roscommon County Library Service

**WITHDRAWN
FROM STOCK**

To Carolyn, for her lasting friendship
and her amazing medical facts!

Special thanks go to:

Lee, a wonderful pilot, who advised me on
all things aviation, and gave me a gorgeous
helicopter ride over Sydney Harbour.

Steve, from Bogong Horseback Adventures,
for his poetic description of horse riding
in the snow.

Catherine, for the idea of riding horses
in the snow.

Roscommon County Library Service

WITHDRAWN
FROM STOCK

CHAPTER ONE

'Is HE always late?'

'He's a doctor, Meg.' The pilot gave her a wry smile.

'*Now* you tell me, Tom!' She tried to laugh but her frustration strangled it. Standing on the tarmac with icy wind whipping her, she shielded her eyes and peered into the late-afternoon, winter sun, willing the other passenger they were waiting for to appear from behind the hangar.

She wanted to get home. She'd had her fill of Melbourne, five days in the 'Big Smoke' was long enough. Now she couldn't wait to get back to the farm nestled in the Australian Alps, back to her job at the bush nursing centre, and back to check on her mother.

'There he is.' Tom pointed and moved toward

a tall man, who had a ski bag slung casually over one broad shoulder and a travel bag on the other.

An irrational irritation zipped through her at the sight of the skis. She reminded herself that not all skiers were rich and obnoxious. Not all skiers were Graeme.

She watched, with the sun blurring their features, as the two men shook hands, and Tom relieved the doctor of the travel bag.

They walked toward her. To her horror she felt herself giving the passenger the once-over. His impressive height she'd noticed immediately but now he was closer she saw his chestnut hair, streaked with blond, kicking up behind his ears. To match that dishevelled look he had a two-day stubble, which outlined firm lips. Lips that suddenly curved upwards, along with his dark brows.

Hell, she'd been caught scoping him out.

'Meg, this is Dr Cameron,' Tom called out over his shoulder as he walked past to stow the skis into the wing lockers and the luggage into the back of the light plane. He secured it all with a mesh safety harness.

'Call me Will.' The man's deep voice wrapped

around her like hot chocolate on caramel. He smiled and stuck out his hand.

His large warm hand enveloped her cooler one, his heat transferring itself to her palm. But it didn't stop there. It wove up her arm and deep into her body. Heat and tingles. Heat and quivers.

The delicious sensations unnerved her. It was the end of a long week, she was tired and cold, so of course she'd shiver. Her body was too tired to know what it was doing and was getting all its signals wrong. 'Pleased to meet you, Will. I'm Meg Watson.'

'Sorry to have kept you waiting in the cold, Meg.'

She looked up into hazel-green eyes ringed by long, thick black lashes—lashes most women would have killed to have. Kind eyes. Eyes that gazed into your soul.

'Right, you two, get on board.' Tom called them over.

'Guess we better do as we're told.' Will grinned and released her hand. 'After you.'

Her hand suddenly felt colder than before she'd met him, and she resisted the urge to shove it into her pocket. She stepped up onto the metal disc that was the step into the light plane. Holding on to the side of the doorway, she ducked her head, hauling herself into the familiar eight-seater plane. Except today there were only two seats for passengers, the rest of the space taken up with brown boxes. She sat down and immediately buckled her seat belt.

Tom did freight and passenger runs between the high country and Melbourne, and had done so for the last thirty years. Meg had known him all her life, and when Tom had insisted on flying her home from the nursing conference, she'd been happy to accept. The flight was a lot quicker than seven hours on the bus and she was desperate to get home.

Will's height and bulk filled the plane as he brushed past and swung into the opposite seat, his long legs seeming to concertina into the cramped space. He smiled at her, his eyes crinkling at the edges. 'I think they design these things for people less then six feet tall.'

She ignored the fluttering sensation that skipped along her veins at his smile. 'She's small but sturdy.'

'Yep, Tom loves this plane, that's for sure.'

Long, tanned fingers dexterously snapped his seat belt into place across his lap, their actions mesmerising Meg.

'Tom's been flying me to Mt Hume since I was a kid.' He gave a sharp tug to tighten the belt, and turned slightly to face her. 'So the snow report is looking fantastic. We're in for a great weekend with all that soft powder in the back country.' Enthusiasm and anticipation wove through his voice.

Meg swallowed a sigh. If Will Cameron had been flying to Mt Hume since he was a kid then he'd been some rich kid. And it seemed the tradition continued—now he was a rich skiing adult. He represented the demographic Meg's home town needed yet disliked. Laurelton depended on the money skiers brought into the town, but too often the skiers used and abused the hospitality. Used and abused the fragile alpine environment.

Used and abused the locals. Meg knew the story personally. Graeme had taught her well and had left a legacy to permanently remind her. Chlamydia's detritus—infertility.

Meg's smile felt tight and forced across her cheeks. 'I'm sure you'll have a great weekend.' She turned slightly and rummaged in her handbag for some peppermints, hoping Will would take the hint and end the conversation. Skiers belonged to a different world from her. A world she'd once tried to visit. A world in which she'd never fit. She belonged at the base of the mountain where the air wasn't quite as rarefied.

'You're not skiing, then?' Curiosity moved across his handsome face, trailing down high cheekbones and along a strong jaw.

'No.' She knew she was verging on rudeness but she didn't want to talk to this man who made her heart hammer. A man from the world she vowed she'd never enter again.

'Ah, you're a snowboarder.' He grinned. 'Sorry, of course, a young woman like yourself wouldn't do anything as boring as skiing.'

His grin was infectious and she laughed. 'It's nothing to do with the snowboarding-ski rivalry. I live in Laurelton. I'm going home.' Her voice softened on the last word.

He smiled knowingly. 'A place you love. How long have you lived there?'

'All my life, with the exception of the five years I spent in Melbourne getting enough work experience so I could return.'

He nodded. 'I can understand why you're keen to get back to Laurelton. I've always loved the town. The post office clock stands like a beacon when you round the final bend and cross the old wooden bridge.' He laughed. 'Of course, the wonky neon sign at Nick's hamburger joint tends to be the night beacon. It never seems to be able to flash NICK all at once.'

Surprise rushed into Meg and she looked into his face, stunned to see an expression of fondness for her town. 'That sign's never worked properly.'

'Yeah, I remember when it went up I was about fourteen. Occasionally Dad would drive up the mountain, usually to test out the latest four-wheel-drive, and I loved those trips.' He smiled at the memory. 'Having Dad's undivided attention was a rarity. Anyway, we'd stop for a snack on the way. I can still taste Nick's hamburger with the lot—pineapple, egg, beetroot…' His voice trailed off and he licked his lips.

Her gaze riveted itself to his mouth as his tongue rolled over the apex of his top lip. Her breathing stalled. *What are you doing?* Sanity prevailed and she dragged her gaze away, staring out the window, thankful Tom had started the propellers.

The noise of the engines drowned out any conversation without the aid of headsets. She noticed out of the corner of her eye Will putting his headset on but she held back, leaving hers in her lap.

He was a doctor heading away for the weekend, excited and chatty. Nothing more, nothing less. Once they landed he would head further up the mountain and she would head down, back to her real life, which was a world away from his.

Will took a surreptitious look at Meg, who was winding her headset through her hands in a rolling motion. He wanted her to put the headset on over her riot of strawberry blonde curls so he could keep talking to her. Except she didn't seem too keen to talk to him.

It wasn't often he had to work hard to get a conversation going—usually he was the one trying to be polite but cool. Generally, just the mention of his name sparked recognition in the eyes of the person he was being introduced to, and the men pumped his hand extra hard and the women began flirting. The Cameron wealth did that to people.

But Meg Watson's luminous baby-blue eyes hadn't glinted at the words 'Will Cameron'. And as for flirting, hell, she'd hardly looked at him since their introduction. But when she had it had been as if she'd shot a bolt of lightning out of her eyes, stunning him.

Suddenly this trip to the mountain had taken on a new dimension. Meeting Meg had immediately lightened his mood about this work trip. He'd hoped she might be on the mountain this week because spending time skiing with a gorgeous woman like Meg, a woman who didn't know about him, would give him some welcome anonymity. It would make up for the rest of the week.

The week he'd spend convincing Jason Peters to commit $100,000 to St Jude's Hospital building fund. Will sighed. Sometimes the old school tie came in handy. But it came at a cost. He knew the type of people who would be the other guests at Jason's ski-in, ski-out apartment.

The sort of people he'd grown up surrounded by—wealthy, pampered and insular. Funny, he'd always had a better rapport with his patients, who came from all walks of life, than most of his parents' friends and their children. But for the sake of his patients he'd use his childhood connections.

Tom's voice came through the headset. 'Estimated flight time is fifty minutes. The weather's predicted to change but, based on the radar, we should get in well before that happens.'

The small plane charged down the runway, its nose rising quickly under Tom's experienced hand. Will leaned back and relaxed. He'd done this flight four to five times a year since the age of five and he always got a kick out of the different cargos Tom carried. This time of year it was usually other skiers but today it was fresh fruit and vegetables, caviar and champagne. Someone on the mountain was throwing a party.

Meg popped a mint into her cherry-red mouth,

her plump lips closing behind it. Desire flared in Will, leaving stunned surprise in its wake. Since Taylor's betrayal six years ago he'd doggedly avoided women, although they didn't avoid him. Just like Taylor, the women he met generally had dollar signs in their eyes. Amazing how money could produce a declaration of love.

Wealth reduced marriage to a business contract. Despite numerous women having other ideas, he had no plans to be part of any relationship.

Instead, in Cameron tradition, he threw himself into work, even though it wasn't exactly the job of his heart. At least the Cameron wealth was being put to good use, raising money for medical facilities and research.

'Would you like a mint?' Meg's melodic voice came through his headset.

He turned to find her fine tapered fingers holding a container of mints toward him.

The plane hit an air pocket. Her hand moved with the jolt, colliding with his thigh, sending waves of hot sensation down his leg and mints cascading into his lap.

She laughed, a tinkling, infectious laugh.

'Sorry.' In a typical 'I can fix it' action, she reached for the mints, her fingers lightly caressing his lap as she scooped up the sweets.

Colours exploded in his head and he breathed in deeply, reciting the monotonous eight-times table, something he hadn't needed to do since he'd been sixteen.

'It's fine, really, I'll fix it.' He heard an unfamiliar huskiness in his voice.

Her hand paused, hovering above his lap, and then it shot back to her own. Her gasp of realisation sounded in his headset. Her cheeks burned red. 'Sorry.' This time embarrassment clung to the word.

She pivoted away and stared resolutely out the window, her discomposure evident. He bagged the remaining offending mints and wished he was out on the slopes, in the cold. His libido, which had been dormant for some time, needed some alpine air to cool it down.

Oh, God! Meg knew eggs could be fried on her cheeks. What had she *not* been thinking when she'd tried to pick up those mints?

She shook her head and kept her gaze fixed firmly out the window. Not that she could see that much as the brilliant blue sky had become overcast. The gaps between the clouds became shorter and less frequent, and a huge cumulonimbus cloud loomed ahead. Grey black, thunderous and full of snow. Must be the weather Tom had mentioned coming in.

She sat up a bit straighter and nibbled her bottom lip. She didn't like the look of that cloud at all.

'We'll take a bit longer than usual because of the head wind, folks.' Tom's voice broke into her thoughts.

A few moments later, rain started to trickle down the windowpane, the droplets looking like fat tadpoles. A flicker of anxiety skated along her veins. She quickly reminded herself that flying in rain was safer than driving a car in it.

She glimpsed the snow line and relaxed. Pretty soon Tom would be circling to bring the plane in to land. And fifteen minutes after that she'd be home, having a hot cup of tea and checking that her mother had not overdone things while she'd been away.

Meanwhile, she gazed out at the tall, straight snow gums, their shiny dark green leaves creating a thick canopy. Thank goodness for national parks. It was hard to imagine that this whole alpine area had once been densely treed just like this, barely a space to glimpse the snow on the ground.

The airstrip abutted the national park and she heard Tom on the radio, talking to the resort's control tower about the landing and giving their position. She could smell home.

Cold started to seep into her and she pulled on her jacket. Although she loved this little plane, there were times she felt like she was inside a tin can. The outside temperature was often reflected inside.

'Right, folks, we'll be there in ten minutes. We could be in for a bit more turbulence but I've been given clearance and we should make it in ahead of the storm. Meg, you might want to grab that sick bag.' Tom turned and gave her a cheeky grin.

Once she'd been sick and, although it had been more to do with bad take-away chicken than a rough flight, Tom loved to tease her about it.

Roscommon County Library Service

WITHDRAWN FROM STOCK

'You OK?'

A thread of warmth spun inside her at the sound of Will's smooth, deep voice. She looked up and nodded. 'Fine. Thanks. And you?'

Argh! What was wrong with her? Now she couldn't even sound coherent, her words coming out in a staccato beat. She focused on the rain.

Suddenly, the plane lurched violently and her seat belt pulled against her, pinning her to her seat.

Hail pounded the plane, balls of ice battering metal, the noise deafening, like bullets on a target. Fear sliced through Meg, her heart pounding so hard she thought it would bound out of her chest. Without thinking, she reached over and gripped Will's arm.

Immediately his hand covered hers, steadying her.

'He's an experienced pilot.' His hazel-green eyes, flecked with topaz, held her gaze, but his hand tightened around hers.

The smoothness of the engines suddenly sounded rough. Meg's heart seemed to stop as dread rushed through her like white water through a gorge. *You're just imagining engine trouble.* She forced her mind to think of tranquil rainforests. *It will be OK.*

Will's hand tensed on hers.

Across his shoulder she saw ice forming on the window.

Ice!

Surely that was just a build-up of hail? She prayed it was. Ice on the wings wasn't good. Planes didn't fly well when ice weighed them down.

Engines didn't like ice either.

She turned and focused on Tom's back, feeling impotent. She watched his every action as if that would help them through the storm. Could he keep the carburettor warm, keep the ice at bay? Could he see the horizon? Could he see the ground?

She couldn't see anything out her window. Nothing but grey fog.

Her heart hammered, sounding loud in her ears. The hail pounded the fuselage. All the noise combined, making her want to put her hands over her ears like a child. Her breath stalled, fear paralysing her lungs.

And then silence.

The hail had stopped. Her breath rushed out in

one long swoosh. For the briefest moment she relished the peace. ⚘

It's too quiet, the voice screamed in her head, clawing, pounding against her brain. The usually loud, rhythmic piston engines were silent.

She automatically leaned forward, watching Tom, wanting to do something, willing him to do something.

He throttled the engines back and forth, his shoulders rigid.

Meg prayed for a fuel blockage that would be easily fixed by his action.

The silence lingered like a malignant growth.

'Bloody hail. No fuel's getting through the carburettor.' Tom's voice trembled. 'I'm sending out a mayday.'

Fear tore at Meg and she turned to Will. 'But the hail's stopped. I don't understand.'

His handsome face paled but strength lingered. 'The moisture in the air, combined with the drop in temperature, caused the ice. If the engines can't get fuel, they can't restart.'

'Oh, my God.' She knew under this fog lay the national park and her beloved gum trees. But they wouldn't love a plane. They stood firm, strong and too close together to gently receive a plane.

'Mayday, mayday, mayday. Duchess D.A.V. with three POB, ten miles from Laurelton at five thousand feet, heading north. Both engines failed. Do you have me on radar?'

The radio buzzed static.

'Right.' Tom's voice sounded in control again. 'Emergency drill. Tighten your seat belts. I'm turning off the fuel tap and I'm going to glide her down.'

'But you can't see anything!' Terror forced the words everyone knew out of her mouth.

'Meg, love, I don't have any choice.' The finality in his voice sealed her fear.

Meg wanted to run. To jump out of the plane. Anything but stay there and do nothing.

'Put your head down on your knees, Meg.' Will spoke quietly but his voice was laced firmly with control.

Dazed with shock, she followed his instructions, not wanting to let go of his hand, not wanting to let go of his supportive strength, but knowing she needed her hands to cradle and protect her head.

'Let's do it on the count of three.' Will nodded at their clasped hands, understanding the need they both had to stay connected. Knowing they couldn't.

She bit her lip. 'One, two, three.' She let go of his hand and felt the plane dropping through the sky.

'Mayday, mayday, mayday. Duchess D.A.V. with three POB, ten miles from Laurelton at two thousand feet heading north. Both engines failed, do you have me on radar?' The desperation and fear in Tom's voice rang through the plane.

The shudder ripped through her as the plane hit the canopy of trees.

Glass shattered.

Timber splintered.

The crunching noise of ripping, crumpling metal screamed in her ears as her own screams stayed trapped in her throat. She was going to die.

She didn't want to die.

The plane dived forward nose first, the weight pulling it inextricably downward to unforgiving solid ground.

An almighty boom sounded in her ears.

Everything went black.

CHAPTER TWO

BLACK fuzz swirled in Will's brain, confusing him as he stiffened against the pain burning through his body. He dragged his eyes open against a trail of warm blood. A tree protruded through the plane directly in front of him. Vegetables and green glass, the shattered remains of champagne bottles, surrounded him.

He forced himself to think through the fog that clogged his mind, to really focus. He couldn't remember the impact, only the icy fear that had preceded it.

An eerie silence encircled him, broken occasionally by the creaking of the trees.

He turned his head slowly, grateful he could move at all. He flexed his fingers, his arms and his legs. All moved. He breathed in deeply. Knife-sharp pain lanced him.

Ribs. His hand cupped his side. Broken or bruised, he couldn't tell.

He heard a moan.

Meg.

The confused fog lifted instantly.

Meg. Tom. They had to get out of the plane. It could explode, catch fire. His mind started racing. He had to get them out of the plane.

He fumbled for his seat belt and clumsily released the catch. 'Meg?' His hand gripped her shoulder and gave it a gentle shake.

She swivelled around, her gaze resting on him, her face blanched white but scarred red by blood. She opened her mouth. No words came out.

'Can you move?' He gently released her seat belt.

'I…I don't know… I…'

Hell, she was shocked. He needed her brain to kick back in like his had. 'We have to get out of the plane, Meg. Now.' He used her name. Shocked people responded to their name. 'Meg, can you move your legs?'

She wriggled her toes. She stretched out her legs. 'I can.'

'Good. I'm going to help you stand up.' He put his arm under her shoulder, biting his lip against his own pain as she pulled forward and stood. She grimaced as her ankle took her weight.

'Tom.' She looked around wildly, her view obscured by the tree. 'Tom.' Her voice rose frantically.

'Meg.' Will continued to grip her arm and locked his gaze with hers. 'We have to get out of the plane on this side of the tree and then we'll get to Tom.'

Her blue eyes, dull since the crash, suddenly cleared to the vivid blue he'd so admired when he'd first met her. Her head snapped around, taking in her surroundings. The tree had come through the side of the plane where the door had been. 'We'll have to kick out the back emergency exit.'

He nodded. 'I'll do it. Your ankle shouldn't kick anything.'

Clambering over the freight toward the tail of the plane, glad he was wearing his hiking boots, he swung a kick at the exit. The metal gave way and he slithered out. Enormous snowflakes tumbled onto him and cold air bit his skin. He breathed in, praying to smell only fresh alpine air.

He got a lungful of aviation fuel. Dread clawed back. Hell, he only hoped the snow fell heavily enough to put out any sparks. Hoping that if the plane was going to explode, it would have done so by now. The engines had given out a couple of minutes before they'd crashed so they probably weren't hot enough to catch fire on impact.

Still, he wanted out.

He leaned back into the plane. 'Meg.' He held out his arms.

She crawled toward him and he heaved her through the gap, his ribs screaming as she fell against him. For a brief moment he held her tight, needing to feel her heart hammering against his chest. Needing to know they both lived, they had both survived.

Clutching her tightly and trying to hold off the fear that Tom was dead.

'Tom. Go to Tom.' She pushed him away and turned back, leaning into the plane to reach for something. 'I'll send up the emergency flares.'

He ran forward, snow biting into his eyes,

ignoring the fire of pain in his side. The plane had dived nose first, the front section taking the impact. Tom was strapped in his seat but the seat had moved forward, wedging him against the controls. He sat still, his head slumped sideways covered in blood.

It looked as if his face had hit the control panel on impact and then whipped back. His jaw sagged, probably broken, along with his nose, which looked crushed.

And they were the injuries Will could see. Hauling the pilot's door open, he yelled, 'Tom.'

No response. He put his first two fingers on Tom's neck, feeling for the carotid pulse.

A weak and thready beat pulsed under his finger pads. Tom needed to be out of plane a.s.a.p. but moving him without a neck brace risked paraplegia. He didn't have a neck brace so his choice was limited. Alive but paralysed? Or dead?

Will hated triage.

'Is he alive?'

Will swung around at the sound of Meg's terrified voice to see her clutching a large black backpack, a tarpaulin and coats.

An overwhelming need to protect her surged inside him. 'Get back. I don't need you being blown up if the plane explodes.'

'And how are you going to get him out on your own? Don't be ridiculous.' The terrified tone had been replaced with an 'in-charge' voice. She shoved the coat and gloves at him. 'Put this on, I don't need you getting hypothermia. You're a doctor, you know the risk.'

To his complete amazement she hauled out a soft neck brace from the black pack. 'Here, put this on Tom and then we can carry him in the tarp.'

He grabbed the proffered brace. 'Are you Mary Poppins? What else have you got in that bag?'

'It's the new emergency pack I picked up at the medical and nursing conference I was coming home from. Laurelton Bush Nursing Centre needed one, but I wasn't expecting to use it so soon.'

'You're a nurse and you've got an 'in-the-field' emergency medical kit?' Incredulity overtook him.

'Yes.'

His panic dropped back a notch. 'Thank God for that.' He swung back to his patient. 'Tom, I'm putting on a neck brace and we're going to get you out of here.'

Tom groaned as Will put the brace around his neck.

He should check for fractures in the pilot's arms and legs but he had no splints to use and the fear of the plane catching fire grew by the moment. Will just wanted him out.

Then he could examine him. Know what he was really up against.

'Meg, we'll have to roll him out together.'

'I'm right here. Just tell me what you want me to do.'

The strength in her voice transferred itself to him. 'Spread the tarp out and then come and support his neck while I lower the back of the seat.'

Meg moved in close, her small hands dextrously holding Tom's head and neck. Her light floral scent enveloped Will, defying the horror of their situation.

He tugged on the seat lever, praying it would work. The seat back started to move and he gently lowered it so Tom was lying flat.

The pilot's breathing became noisy.

Will fought the desire to treat him there and then. But he couldn't risk three lives. They had to get away from the plane. 'You control his head and neck and I'll look after the rest. On my count, we roll.' He positioned himself so he could control the large man's legs.

'One, two, three.' He pulled hard, his ribs blazing with pain. Together they rolled Tom as carefully as possible, given the situation, onto the tarp.

Meg limped to the other side of the tarp, rolling the edges in as close to Tom as possible. 'Will one hundred metres away be safe enough?'

'Should do it. Give me that pack and I'll wear it. You'll struggle enough carrying Tom.'

She tilted her head, her cheeks pink from cold and exertion. 'I've seen you flinch. Your ribs are bruised or broken. We'll put the pack next to Tom so we can both manage.'

He wanted to argue but couldn't. Not with logic like that. 'One, two, three, lift.' He grunted and lifted, moving forward slowly. With each step he sank knee deep into powder snow. Exhaustion dragged at him.

With every step, Meg grimaced with pain. He

adjusted his grip on the tarp, trying to take more of the load. He pushed on, hoping Tom would still be alive when they got to the clearing Meg had picked out.

'On my count, down.' Meg's arms shook with exhaustion as she lowered Tom onto the snow.

Will dropped to his knees and checked the pilot's pulse. Weak.

'Here.' Meg handed him a stethoscope and an LED headlamp, while she ripped open a space blanket package with her teeth.

It was surreal. All this medical gear belonged in A and E, not in the middle of an alpine national park.

Meg covered Tom, the snow falling white against the silver blanket.

Tom's respirations had worsened—loud, gurgly and noisy. Bubbles of blood formed in his mouth.

Will checked his air entry with the stethoscope. 'Shallow resps, poor air entry.'

'Pneumothorax from the joystick?'

He examined Tom's face. 'Possibly, but he's got a severely fractured maxilla. The middle of his face has separated from the rest.' He looked up at her. 'All this bleeding and swelling isn't helping his breathing.'

Understanding crossed her face. 'Do you need to do a tracheostomy?'

'Yes, we need to establish his airway if we've got any chance of keeping him alive.'

'And risk paralysis if his spinal cord is damaged.' She bit her lip. 'I hate triage.'

'You're not alone there.' They were between a rock and a hard place. The treatment to save Tom's life could render his life changed for ever.

'Do you have a wide-bore needle, a fourteen-gauge, in that pack?'

Meg frantically scanned the laminated sheet. 'I can do better than that.' She read out the instructions. 'In large bottom pouch, tracheostomy tube.' Her fingers, pink with cold, fumbled as she opened the pack.

'That's one hell of a kit.' Will took off his coat, rolling it up under Tom's shoulders to extend the pilot's neck. He removed the soft brace. 'Tom, we have to put a tube into your throat. You won't be able to talk.' He had no idea if Tom could hear him. He was pretty certain he was unconscious.

She handed him the scalpel and cleaned Tom's throat with the antiseptic wipe. 'How long since you've done a trachy?'

Will didn't lie. 'On an adult, it's been a long time.'

'Some things you never forget.' She gave him an encouraging smile, her confidence in him almost palpable.

He found the cricoid cartilage. *The trachea is generally two finger-breadths above the sternal notch.* The words of his surgical professor pounded in his head. He made a horizontal cut through the skin, the muscle and down into the cartilage of the trachea.

Meg tried to keep the area free of blood so he could see.

He needed to find the third or fourth ring of cartilage. 'Pass the tube.'

He pressed firmly on the tracheostomy tube, until the resistance disappeared and the tube was *in situ.*

'You inflate the balloon to keep the tube in place and I'll check his breathing.'

He lifted the space blanket and put the

stethoscope on Tom's chest. The pilot didn't flinch at the cold. Not a good sign. 'His air entry is better but his pulse is weak. Open facial fractures bleed like hell. He's lost a bucket of blood.'

'Do you want me to bag him?'

'Yes. I'll see if I can get an IV in. What have you got?'

'One litre of Hartmann's solution.'

An expletive rose to his lips. One thousand millilitres wouldn't replace the circulating volume Tom had lost.

'It's better than nothing, Will.'

Meg's voice of reason penetrated his fear and frustration. 'You're right—sorry.'

As she rhythmically squeezed the air bag he tried desperately to find a vein. Tom was in severe shock, his veins collapsed. Will tightened the tourniquet around Tom's arm. His fingers desperately palpated for a raised vein. Nothing.

He moved the tourniquet three times, trying arms and legs. Still nothing. He sucked in a deep breath, forcing himself to concentrate and to ignore the dread that curled in his belly.

'Do a venous cutdown.' Meg's desperate words echoed his thoughts. 'We've got a scalpel.'

The natural light was almost gone. In the glow of his headlamp he saw her face streaked with blood and pain, yet there was a steely determination there. She wasn't giving in without a hell of a fight.

Neither was he.

'You keep bagging and I'll do the cutdown.' His fingers, now half-numb with cold, seemed clumsy but he managed to make a clean cut and locate the vein. The wide-bore cannula slid in and he attached the IV, turning it on full bore. He only hoped it wouldn't be running straight out of Tom's body.

'Put your gloves on.' Meg's voice had a schoolteacher-like quality. 'I don't need you getting frostbite.' Her voice cracked slightly on the last word.

Her concern touched him. 'How are you doing?'

She bit her lip. 'Fine.'

But he knew she was far from it. None of them were fine. Snow covered her hat and coat and her cheeks burned red from the cold.

An icy feeling crept through him. The temperature was dropping fast now the sun was down. Hypothermia was a real issue and they needed some sort of shelter, but attempting to get Tom stable had to come first. 'You know, the cold might count in our favour.'

Meg shivered. 'How?'

'The cold slows down the heart rate and the metabolic process. Perhaps it will slow down Tom's bleeding.'

'Good, because his pulse is getting weaker.' Her voice wobbled with alarm.

Will examined Tom's abdomen and chest. Air was going in and his respirations were easier with the tracheostomy. But his abdomen was guarded, a sure sign of internal bleeding. He'd bet his bottom dollar Tom's heart was pumping the lifesaving Hartmann's solution straight into his peritoneum. It was no use to him there.

Worse still, there was nothing Will could do to stop it. Tom needed to be evacuated to a trauma centre urgently, only that wasn't going to happen.

'Are you sure there is only Hartmann's?' Will

scrounged through the pack, praying for more IV fluids.

'I'm O-negative.' Meg gave him a knowing look. 'We could do a direct blood transfusion.'

Again, the protective surge moved in him, strong and hard. 'No way. It's far too dangerous for you.'

'Tom's like a father to me.' Her voice rose. 'We have to do all we can.'

He respected her courage, her desire to do all at whatever cost. 'We are doing all we can. But without surgery to stem his internal bleeding, your blood will just end up pooling in his abdomen. More importantly, you could get a blood-borne illness. You know direct blood transfusions stopped years ago.'

'I'm fit. I can handle it.' Her jaw jutted in defiance of the conditions, the situation. With her free hand she reached for an IV line.

But he saw a sliver of fear streak across her face.

'Being fit is irrelevant against hepatitis C.' He touched her arm, hoping to show her he understood her feeling of impotence at the situation. Her fear. 'Let's see if the Hartmann's brings up his blood pressure.'

But he was certain it was too late for that.

Will took over the bagging, letting Meg dress Tom's gaping wounds. She needed to do something, needed to claw back some control in a situation that had none.

He surveyed the towering trees. Now the wind had dropped, the snow fell straight down. The pink of sunset reflected through the snowflakes. Under other circumstances, being out in the bush with a beautiful woman, with snow falling quietly around them, would be magical.

But now was far from magical. How would the rescuers find them in such dense bush?

'Tom.' Meg spoke quietly. 'I've sent up the flares, they know we're here. They'll find us.' She placed packing gauze against his crushed nose.

She glanced up at the Hartmann's bag, now almost empty. 'How's his BP?'

'Dropping.' He hated this. Hated watching a man's life drain away in front of him. 'I'm sorry, Meg, we can't do any more. We tried.' His voiced trailed off, the words sounding inadequate.

Her wide-eyed distress sliced into him.

She gripped Tom's hand and dropped her

head down next to his ear. 'When Dad died, you were there. You've been such source of strength to me and Mum. Thank you.' Her voice cracked. 'I love you.'

Tom's pulse faded to nothing under Will's fingertips. 'He's gone, Meg.'

For a brief moment her shoulders shuddered. Then she leaned forward and kissed Tom's forehead. She pulled the space blanket aside, putting it behind her. Taking the corners of the tarp, she folded them over him, wrapping Tom's body completely, carefully protecting his body from the continuous snowfall. Then she reached over and grabbed a large stick. Pushing it into the snow, she marked Tom's position.

Each action spoke of love and the desolation on her face pierced Will. He moved toward her almost unthinkingly, pulled her to her feet and into his arms. She fell against him, her chest shuddering with suppressed tears, her arms gripping his. He wanted to comfort her, hold her tight against him and ease her grief. Tell her he was so very sorry they couldn't do any more.

But there was no time for that.

He moved back slightly so he could see her face. He needed to make eye contact. Needed to see those sky-blue eyes, now cloudy with grief, clear.

He was strong, but he knew the odds. They were stranded, miles from help, in harsh conditions. Damn it, he needed the 'take charge' Meg back or they wouldn't get through this alive.

Tom was dead.

The pitch black of the alpine night cloaked her along with the heavily falling snow. For one brief moment she'd given in to her grief and found solace cuddled against Will's broad chest, feeling his heart beating against her own.

But then he'd moved away.

'Meg, we need to take shelter before we freeze.'

He'd spoken to her. The words, distant at first, suddenly sounded louder. Will's voice penetrated her fudge-like brain and Meg looked up into his face.

By the light of his headlamp she could see congealed blood on his dark eyebrow from a deep gash. Scratches hid in the stubble of his dark beard, the only hint of their presence tiny clots of blood. She wanted to reach out and touch them. Offer comfort.

'You need steri-strips on your eyebrow.' Her voice was husky.

He gave a wry smile. 'You can be the first-aid queen as soon as we get some shelter.' His gloved hands gripped her forearms firmly, his energy seeming to flood her, giving her back the strength she'd just lost.

Shelter.

He was right—they'd freeze without shelter. The wind chill had sent the temperature way below zero. 'Will the plane be safe?'

'No, it's too risky with all that aviation fuel. We didn't get this far to be blown up. By morning it will be OK but for now we need to construct some sort of lean-to.'

She shook her head. 'Snow cave.'

'What?'

'We need to make a snow cave to protect us from this icy wind.' She glanced around, taking in the area. It was so dark she couldn't see a thing. Where the hell was the moon when you needed it? 'Can you move your head around so I can see the area?'

He moved in close to her and bent his knees so his head was level with hers. Putting his arm around her, he slowly propelled her 360 degrees, the small beam of light exposing the area.

She wanted his arm, his warmth, to stay with her. But that was impossible. 'Over there.' She pointed to a large snowdrift. 'We can dig a compartment big enough for the two of us and use bracken to cover ourselves. I chucked some gear well clear of the plane so we could go back for that. There might be something we can use.'

'Right now it's too cold and windy and I don't trust that aviation fuel. I don't suppose that medical pack of yours runs to a shovel, does it, Mary Poppins?' A weary grin creased his stubbled cheeks.

Heat coursed through her, stunning her. Despite her throbbing ankle, her bruised body, her heart-ache and her fear, his smile managed to fire up feelings she'd pushed away long ago. Feelings she'd locked down after Graeme had left.

'No shovel, but I could use the face masks to dig with.'

'You plan to dig this cave yourself, do you?' His voice held a slight edge.

Every movement cost him pain—even in the shadowy dark she could see that. He deserved a break after all he'd done, trying to save Tom. 'My ribs aren't bruised or broken. I've seen you grimace with every lift and sudden movement.'

He grunted. 'I'm not alone there. You can hardly walk. Let's just dig the damn cave so we can both rest.' He fell to his knees and started digging.

She sighed. She'd upset him, trying to help him. Graeme had accused her of being far too independent and not playing the 'societal game'. That was another reason why she belonged at the base of the mountain with the farmers who treated their partners as equals.

She shrugged, carefully knelt beside him and handed him a mask. Silently, they dug side by side, developing an unspoken rhythm, alternating the scooping out and dumping of the snow, slowly hollowing out space where they could both sit.

An hour later, warm from the physical work, Meg crawled into the snow cave. She'd dumped the contents of the medical kit at the back of the cave and flattened the backpack to sit on.

Will crawled in next to her, the small space contracting even more. Her heart seemed to flip in her chest. Just like on the plane, his presence unnerved her, but this time she couldn't ignore him. This time his presence would help her survive.

He piled the bracken and tree-fern fronds up at the front and then turned and sat next to her. 'I think this cave might get an architectural award.' His lightning-quick grin streaked across his face as he settled next to her, and then he turned off the headlamp.

'Creative use of minimal space?' She tucked the space blanket around them both as his thigh came to rest against hers.

'Natural heating.' He put his arm around her waist and pulled her gently toward him, closing the tiny space between them.

A blaze of heat flared inside her, which she tried to squash. He was only cuddling her to prevent hypothermia.

'Modern furnishings.' She patted the backpack,

trying to ignore the slight pressure of his hand on her waist.

'Look, we've even got natural light.' He pointed to the moon low on the horizon, rising slowly.

'So we have.' The words came out on a sigh as she looked at the moonlight that had come too late, and thought of Tom.

He squeezed her arm. 'We'll find him in the morning.' His low voice vibrated with under-standing. 'You marked where he was.'

How had he known she was thinking of Tom? She blinked back the tears that hovered ready to spill, the events of the evening threatening to overtake her. 'The morning…' Her voice trailed away.

'Meg, the morning will come and the rescuers will come. You know that. The flares went up and Tom gave the co-ordinates over the radio before we went down. They *will* find us.'

'But not tonight.'

'No, not tonight. They've got no hope of finding us in this storm, and they'd be risking their lives at the same time.'

Damn it, he was right. 'These drifts will be

twice the height in the morning if this snow keeps up. They'll have to come in on horseback first.'

'True, but those mountain men know what they're doing. Even Banjo Patterson knew that. They will come.'

She smiled at his reference to *The Man From Snowy River*, and in the dark of the cave she let his voice infuse her with some of his strength.

She so wanted to relax into him, rest her head on his chest, feel and hear his heart beating. Affirming life. Proof that they had survived the crash, that together they would survive the night.

But that would be weak and she couldn't be weak, so she sat ramrod stiff. She'd learned the hard way that the only person she could depend on was herself. Snowstorm or not, nothing would change that. She knew that once the rescuers arrived she and Will would go their separate ways, strangers again.

She just had to get through the night.

CHAPTER THREE

'TELL me where you learned about snow caves.' Will jostled Meg with his shoulder, hoping to keep her awake.

The cave mostly protected them from the wind but it was bitterly cold. Hypothermia and sleep didn't look very different from the outside. They'd got this far, and he was determined they would make it through the night alive.

She yawned. 'You're trying to keep me awake, aren't you?' A smile played in her voice.

An image of her high cheekbones framing her plump upturned lips flittered across his mind. The same smile that had captivated him six hours ago. It seemed a lifetime ago.

'You've found me out. We don't have to talk about snow caves, we can pick any topic at all.'

A blast of wind brought in snow and he started to cough, his ribs sending out shards of red-hot pain.

She stiffened against him. 'Will?' Her concern radiated through the confined space. She reached out, fumbled with the zipper on his coat and then determinedly searched under his polar fleece until her hand rested on his skin. On his ribs.

Her touch should have been cold. But her fingers sparked off a series of mini-explosions that travelled straight to his groin. Hell! It was below zero, he'd just survived a plane crash, he was in a snow cave with bruised ribs and he could still get aroused. This definitely wasn't the right time or place.

A moan escaped his lips.

He heard her breath catch before her words rushed out. 'You're in pain. Can you breathe without pain?'

'Yes, I can. It just hurts to cough.'

'Are you sure? Please, don't put on a macho act for me. I don't need you developing a punc-tured lung.' The stern tone in her voice couldn't hide her fear.

He wanted to reassure her, lessen her fear, that

he wasn't going to die. That she wouldn't be alone in the snow. 'Think, Meg. If it was worse than bruised ribs, I wouldn't have been able to lift Tom and dig a cave. I've seen your nursing skills in action, you know your stuff. Don't let panic override your knowledge base.'

Her hand dropped away from his skin and the icy air swooped in, absorbing the heat in a moment. 'Sorry.'

'Hey.' He squeezed her shoulder. 'We're in this together and I appreciate your concern. How's your ankle feeling?'

'It's throbbing.'

'Any pins and needles?' He was worried swelling might be impeding blood flow.

'No, I can still feel my toes, so that's a good sign.'

She relaxed slightly, her body resting fractionally more against his. Despite the fact their sides were touching for the much-needed heat exchange, he could feel her holding herself aloof from him.

'So back to snowcaves…' he prompted.

'At high school I did outdoor education. As we're in an alpine region we did both snow and bushfire safety to cover each end of the spectrum. I never expected to use it.'

She wriggled against him in an unconscious action as she tried to get comfortable.

He closed his eyes against the surge of heat that rocketed through him. She had no idea what she did to him and she couldn't know. Tonight they had to keep warm and that meant body contact. He wished he'd taken more notice when his secretary had talked about meditation and achieving a 'Zen-like' state.

She finally stilled, having pulled her legs up to her chin, and he released the breath he hadn't realised he'd been holding. 'So who's worrying about you right now?'

'My mother.' A different tension radiated from her. 'She doesn't need this sort of stress. Mum's got MS. Something like this could spark off a further progression of the disease.'

Regret for her family pulled at him. He knew the emotional toll of a chronically ill parent.

Her hands tugged agitatedly at the space blanket. 'I was worried about her spending this week on her own. I wasn't expecting her to think

I'd died as well.' Her voice rose on the last words, her anxiety palpable.

Professionally he knew she needed to talk, to help keep the panic at bay, and yet part of him wanted to know about her life. 'So, she's still living independently?'

'Yes and no. I live with her and we run the farm together. She gets tired by the end of the day and uses elbow crutches.'

Astonishment combined with admiration. 'You work full-time as a nurse as well as running a farm with an ill mother?'

She nudged him with her elbow. 'You city slickers don't know what hard work is.'

The playful tone in her voice sobered. 'The land is part of you and very hard to give up, no matter the obstacles. And all farmers have those, especially the ones in the Laurel Valley. The bottom dropped out of tobacco a year before Dad died and he'd started to branch out and grow chestnuts. We've kept his phase-one orchard and leased out the rest of the farm to our neighbours.'

'Sounds like tough times.' A niggle of guilt at his financially secure life tweaked him.

'Not just for us. The entire district is struggling. Changing your primary industry after many years of a dropping income is tough. Some people are farming emus, others ostriches, and then, of course, there's tourism.'

He heard her wry tone. 'Tourism brings in the dollars, you can't deny that.'

'You're right, it does, but it changes the town. In winter Laurelton is full of skiers who belt in and belt out. They see the town purely as a service centre and are often very critical of the service. They don't take the time to truly *know* the town, appreciate the area, understand the fragile environment.'

'That's being a bit tough on us, isn't it?'

'Have you ever visited Laurelton out of the snow season?'

Her face was in shadow but he pictured her brows arched in question, her sky-blue eyes flashing in a direct gaze. 'Point taken. I've skied here for years but I've never come at any other time.'

'And you're missing so much!' Her voice became animated. 'There are so many wonderful places that come alive in spring and summer when the snow melts. Tiny orchids grow between rocks, the alpine grass waves in the breeze and the area is dotted with a rainbow of colourful flowers. Only a local can truly show a tourist the real Laurelton, but they don't want to hang around that long.' The passion in her voice for her alpine district filled the cave.

'Do you have any ideas on how to change that?'

'I certainly do.'

He laughed. 'Of course, I should have realised. I'm getting the picture of a very determined woman.'

She shrugged. 'You carve out your own life in this world, and if you don't like something you should set about trying to change it for the better.'

Her words scorched him. Did he do that? He was doing it with his job, trying to improve the lives of sick kids. A voice in his head tried to speak. *Not the way you want to, though.*

He swallowed a sigh. His father's illness had forced both of them to make a career change. But thinking about it didn't change anything. He pushed the uncomfortable thought away as she continued.

'Mum and I run a bed and breakfast and I offer tours of the area all year round between shifts. Mum manages the B&B, although I do a lot of the physical work.'

'So you go from bed-making at work to bed-making at home.' This time he dodged the elbow.

'Cheeky! Although any registered nurse worth her salt knows how to make a patient comfortable, I don't make many beds these days. Mind you, you can learn a lot about a patient, chatting to them while making their bed.'

'You're right. Nurses have that over doctors—the opportunity to talk to patients in a more casual way. It can net you a lot.' But he didn't want to talk about work even though they had medicine in common. He wanted to know more about Meg. 'So you're a farm girl. What about brothers and sisters?'

'I've got two older brothers who were lured by the big city lights. One lives in Sydney, the other in Brisbane. I've always had a stronger connection to the farm and Laurelton. My brothers were born with wanderlust. Me, I'm content where I am.'

'You don't find country life confining?'

She turned to look at him. 'Life confines us wherever we live. Work, family, societal rules. It's how we deal with those confines that count.'

He thought about his family and the social confines their wealth had placed on him when he had been growing up. 'I suppose the confines of family are similar in the city and the country, but here there is less to escape to. Such a small town wouldn't offer, say, a vibrant performing arts scene.'

'True, but I've always got the bush to escape to. Although I could truly do with her being a tad warmer tonight.' Her shiver vibrated against him.

Concern whipped through him. 'Cold? Sorry, dumb question—of course you're cold. How can we change that? We're *not* succumbing to hypothermia.' He mentally ran through their limited options. 'If we face sideways and you sit between my legs and lean back against me, we'll transfer a lot more heat.'

Heat.

And it wouldn't just be cosy heat radiating from him.

The thought of her leaning back into him, her

back resting against his chest, her lower back resting against his lap terrified him.

But this was survival. Nothing more, nothing less.

His wayward libido would just have to deal with it.

Lean back against me.

Meg's breath caught in her throat. Resting back on Will would warm her, but not quite in the way he'd meant. But he was right—they had to try something. It would be hours before they could expect to be rescued. The cold had now invaded her bones, and she was chilled to the core.

Chilled and hungry.

'There isn't much room to turn around in.'

He laughed and again the image of hot chocolate sauce cascading over caramel flooded her. Oh, God, now her imagery was making her hungry.

'If you move forward, I can turn around and arrange the pack. Then I'll move back and you can turn and sit back against me.'

He made it sound so easy. So normal. So very

normal to be stranded in a snowstorm and cuddled up to a total stranger to survive.

A few moments later she sat between Will's legs, the space blanket just reaching around them. Her back ached from sitting upright without support.

His hand burned into her shoulder. 'Meg, lean back. I don't bite, honest.'

No, but *she* might. Her heartbeat quickened as the memory of the feel of his skin under her fingers rushed back. Smooth skin, with taut muscle bands hiding beneath. She'd touched him and now she had a driving urge to taste him.

Oh, God, she'd lost it. This wasn't her, she didn't think like this. She'd sworn off men after Graeme and it was only shock, hunger and fear that were affecting her thoughts.

He gently increased the pressure on her shoulder and she eased back against him, feeling his chest supporting her aching spine.

'Relax, Meg. I can take your weight.'

Relax!

He had no idea. She forced a deep, calming breath into her constricted chest. As she blew the

air out of her lungs she concentrated on letting
her body rest solely on his chest.

'Comfortable?' •

'Yes, thanks.' Was that her voice that squeaked
out the words?

'Great.' His arms encircled her and came to
rest on the tops of her legs in a natural position,
as if they belonged there. Then his chin rested
on her head.

She felt cocooned in a nest of warmth. She
fought the overwhelming urge to totally relax
into his arms. She knew it was pure survival,
there was nothing more to it, but her reaction to
him scared her. The last time she'd given in to a
man, he'd left her. Left her scarred and with
damaged Fallopian tubes. Abandoned her,
leaving only a tattered and useless dream.

The hole in the pit of her stomach growled,
reverberating off the snow walls. 'Sorry, I'm a
bit hungry.'

'When the storm abates, we can get some food
from the plane.'

She grinned. 'It's not all crash survivors who
can claim to have eaten caviar and drunk cham-

pagne while they waited. Although someone on the mountain might have been forced to have supermarket dip and biscuits and—*quelle horreur*—Australian sparkling wine.'

He laughed. 'Ah, but they will incorporate it into a great dinnertime story back in Toorak, which would make up for it.'

'The night they slummed it?'

'Something like that.'

His words carried a reserve she hadn't heard before. Realisation hit her. He was probably talking from experience. She wanted to know. She *needed* to know if her gut feeling about his privileged life was correct. That would be the ammunition she needed to fight her attraction to him. And she must fight it, otherwise it would all end in tears. Her tears.

'You asked who is worrying about me. So, who's worrying about you?'

'I'm guessing that when the plane didn't land the people meeting me will have contacted my parents.'

'Were you staying with family friends?'

'In a manner of speaking, I suppose they are. My

parents certainly consider them family. I've known them all my life, went to school with them.'

A leaden feeling sank in her hungry stomach. Her intuition was correct. 'Old Penton Grammarians?'

'Yes.' Surprise, mixed with an eagerness to establish a shared connection, played though his voice.

She recognised it from Graeme's family and friends. First came the enthusiasm that she was an 'old girl'. Then came the blank 'Oh' when the connection didn't exist.

'Did you go to the sister school?'

Bingo. 'No.' She couldn't keep the edge out of her voice. 'I went to Laurelton Secondary College.' She waited for the 'Oh' and the inevitable silence that followed.

'Didn't Laurelton win the ski cup six to eight years ago? I remember my cousin, James, up in arms that Penton had been outmanoeuvred by a local high school.' He laughed. 'Did them good to learn that even with a truckload of money, you still need skill to win.'

Surprise at his comment wriggled though her.

She was amazed he would remember that. 'We had Stuart McGregor that year. He was a gun skier and went on to represent Australia in the Olympics. But, win or lose, the Penton boys seemed to think it their duty to gatecrash our party. Apparently we were supposed to be grateful for the attention and the fact they added class.' Teenage memories, some tinged with resentment, swirled in her head.

He laughed. 'Yes, some of them could smell a party thirty kilometres away. Although vomiting in the snow never struck me as all that classy.'

'That's true.' Will's answers astonished her. She longed to pigeonhole him but he wasn't quite fitting into the round hole she'd created for him. And her body was betraying her. Her bone-chilling coldness was receding. A bank of heat now permeated her back and she was desperate to press back to soak more of it in. To touch more of him.

With Will's arms cocooning her, his warm breath skating along the edge of her cheeks, the heat from his body surrounding her, she could feel her flimsy walls of defence crumbling. She couldn't let this attraction go anywhere. She had to stop it dead in its tracks.

She drew on what she knew. 'What I don't understand about Penton is why, as adults, old Penton boys want to live in each other's pockets.'

'Security, shared experiences. All the same reasons people hang out in groups.'

'Yes, but...' A niggle of irritation chafed against his reasonableness. 'You have to admit, Penton has made it an art form. It isn't just their ex-schoolmates—they marry the girls from the sister school and then enrol their yet-to-be-conceived children at both schools.' Her words rushed out, carried on a wave of ingrained bitterness and hurt.

'Not all old Penton boys socialise with their schoolmates.' The words seemed clipped.

She heard his change of tone. She'd learned from Graeme that Penton was sacrosanct, above criticism. She'd expected Will to react like that.

Good. She pictured Will slowly morphing into the round shape to fit into the round hole she had all picked out for him. The same hole Graeme had slotted into so well. Money, privilege and a sense of superiority. Use, abuse, move on.

Once she had Will in that hole, her attraction to him would shrivel. 'Yeah, right, weren't you on your way to spend a week with your old school pals?' She squashed the sensible voice in her head that told her she was being childish, sounding petulant. 'I bet you were staying at the Alston, where all good Pentonians stay.' ,

'Actually, I was staying at a private apartment.'

His voice became cool and for the first time she noticed his independent school accent.

A private apartment meant serious money.

Meg knew the mountain like the back of her hand. Each year when a new hotel or apartment complex was built, part of her was pained that fewer ordinary people could afford to enjoy the mountain in the winter. She sat forward and half turned toward him. 'Which apartments?'

'The Grenoble complex.'

She breathed in hard and fast. The Grenoble was the development the local environment group had protested against. *She'd* protested against it. And they'd lost. 'Those apartments should never have been built. Money bought off that planning process. Now the mountain is being taken over and controlled by a select few.'

He tensed behind her. 'Skiing has always been a rich man's sport. There are lodges that provide access to the mountain for people with less money.'

Fury blazed inside her. That was such a 'Graeme' statement. 'Yes, but it's people like you who are driving up the prices for everyone, taking all you want during winter and never giving back.'

'Never give back? We pour hundreds of thousands of dollars into the region, including into Laurelton. We support your livelihoods.'

Face it, Meg. You need my money, you need my connections and you need me. Graeme's smarmy voice boomed in her head.

'That champagne and caviar was probably ordered by your host!' Her voice rose on a wave of anger.

'There is every chance it might have been.' The words were as icy as the cave.

Triumph saluted inside her. She'd been right from the start. Will was in the pigeonhole. Her lust shrivelled. She was safe.

'Do you need me to apologise for that?' He enunciated each word. 'Does being an ex-Pentonian mean I am automatically a lesser person in your eyes?' He paused for a brief moment, his words hanging in the air. 'The fact you don't know anything about me and that you've jumped to a massive stereotype conclusion says more about you than me.'

A kernel of guilt sprouted inside her.

'I don't need to justify myself to you. If you must know, this week's ski trip was as much about work as it was about skiing. This group of rich bastards you so like to malign have the capabilities to donate large amounts of money for research and health-care facilities. Money is tight. The government gives limited amounts and research absorbs money like a bushfire absorbs oxygen. My old school connections come in handy sometimes and I don't apologise for that. I use them to my advantage when I need to.'

An ugly silence settled over them. Meg was physically warm but his words sent shards of ice through her. She'd deliberately been aggressive, so determined to make him the same as Graeme, so determined to protect herself, that she'd been judge and jury with scant evidence.

From the moment they'd met, he'd only been polite and considerate despite the fact she knew she'd been deliberately chilly toward him. He'd put her first so often since the crash, tried to protect her, kept her warm, drawn her out on her life to keep her mind off the situation they found themselves in.

And he was right—she'd jumped to conclusions based on an old festering hurt. She thought she'd moved beyond that pain. Dismay filled her at the knowledge that it still coloured her judgement. She prided herself on being egalitarian but the truth was that since Graeme she no longer trusted. She'd lashed out in self-defence…but she was fighting the wrong person. She needed to be fighting her own prejudice.

'You're right. I'm sorry. I had no right to say those things. I know nothing about you except you ski and you're a doctor.'

His hands balled into fists by his side. 'Apology accepted.'

Yet she knew she wasn't really forgiven. His

tension flowed into her. The relaxed man she'd laughed with earlier had totally disappeared. A sense of having lost something she hadn't even known she wanted settled like a stone inside her.

The longest night of her life had just got longer.

Will swallowed a curse. What had just happened? How had they gone from laughing together to this strained silence? And why had he gone out to bat for his old school when he knew she had a point about some of the past students and their lives?

Hell, he spent enough of his life trying to avoid the type of people she'd described, only attending functions he was obliged to because of his work commitments.

But to have this dynamic woman form an opinion of him and his life based on the actions of a few riled him. And he'd gone in boots and all. He'd heard the sanctimonious tone in his voice, the same cold pitch his house master at Penton had used.

Sounding like him cut him worst of all. He knew the feelings of smallness and guilt that tone generated. He'd heard them in Meg's voice when she'd apologised.

But being right didn't make him feel any better. He was stuck out in the middle of an alpine national park, focusing on survival, yet he let his own discontent eat at him and spill over to taint this gorgeous woman. Life dealt out the cards. Dealing with them was another matter completely.

They passed the rest of the night by playing innocuous games of twenty questions. There'd even been moments when their original camaraderie had briefly reappeared, but Meg sensed a reserve in Will. The flirting doctor had disappeared, gone for ever.

By dawn the wind had dropped and the snow had stopped. The sun rose, a yellow ball in a clear sky, nature almost mocking in its power to change on a penny. Today would have been perfect weather for flying.

'Let's get out of here and stretch.' Will moved away from her and crawled to the entrance, knocking the bracken out of the way.

A deep and intense ache dragged inside her. When she'd been cradled in his arms she'd had moments when she'd hidden from the real world and had fantasised about him wanting her there. But with the dawn she could no longer hide from reality. She realised a person could be cuddled in someone's arms and those arms could be a lonely place when that person didn't care. It was purely a survival tactic. She knew that was all it was, all it would ever be.

It was just her crazy reaction to him that was turning her inside out. Well, the time had come to act like the grown-up she was. 'I'll go fire off more flares now we have a chance of being found. Hopefully the search and rescue team were mobilised to start at first light and will be here soon.'

She followed Will out of the cave, stumbling as her legs adjusted to standing straight after being cramped for so many hours.

His hand caught hers and he steadied her.

'Thanks.' She looked up into his dark eyes, glimpsing concern and something else, which flashed past so quickly it was gone before she could interpret it.

'OK?' His deep voice caressed her.

'I'll be fine, just some pins and needles.' She

spoke too quickly, unnerved by the trail of heat his hand generated.

'What about your ankle?'

'It's down to a dull throb.'

'I guess that's as good as you can hope for.' He started to move forward but caught sight of the stick marking Tom's body. Snow covered three-quarters of its height. He bowed his head and squeezed her hand.

His touch, a light squeeze of comfort, said more than words. Guilt dug in over her behaviour the night before. But now wasn't the place to deal with that. Today's focus had to be getting found.

They trudged back to the plane, silent in their own thoughts. Meg fired off the flares, the flame scarring the clear sky. She sent up a silent prayer, hoping it would not be much longer before they were found.

Snow had covered a lot of the food that she'd pulled from the plane but she found some dry biscuits. With cold, clumsy fingers she opened the box and offered them to Will. 'Let's imagine cheese.' She gave him a weak smile. 'I fancy some runny Camembert.'

His grin, the one she'd memorised and replayed in her head last night while listening to his voice in the dark, split his face. 'Seeing as we're no longer sharing a small space, I reckon I'll go for pungent blue-vein.'

She laughed, enjoying the sensation, appreciating she still had the opportunity to laugh.

'Coo-ee! Coo-ee!' Men's voices rent the air.

Meg spun around toward the sound, the biscuits flying out of the packet.

'Coo-ee!' Will's deep voice resonated around the area.

'Over here! Over here!' Excitement rushed through her. She wanted to jump up and down but her ankle wouldn't let her. Instead, she peered through the trees, hoping to see the rescuers. She turned back to Will, grabbing his arms. 'They're coming, they're really coming.'

'Hurray.' He slung his arm around her waist, his gaze locking with hers. Deep green eyes, flecked with chocolate brown, swirled with relief and exhilaration.

Pure longing rocketed through her, taking her breath away.

He laughed, a deep-throated sound that made her toes curl with desire. Then he pulled her close, her chest resting gently on his. It was as if the layers of polar fleece and coats had disappeared. His heat scorched her.

He brought his hand up to her face and his scent of damp wool, sweat and pine enveloped her. He lowered his head to hers and firmly captured her lips with his.

Surprise and wonder raced through her.

The kiss was ice and fire. Pressure mixed with tenderness. He tasted of salt, cold and fiery heat.

She opened her mouth to welcome him, desperate to taste more of him, wanting to explore, feel, savour.

But as quickly as it had started, the kiss ended. His arms fell away. 'Here!' He started waving his arm in a large arc.

Dazed, Meg turned to see four horses coming through the trees. The rescuers had arrived. She should feel over the moon with relief.

All she could think of was how much life could change in seventeen hours.

CHAPTER FOUR

THE small church was packed to overflowing. After a coroner's inquest, Tom's body was finally released two weeks after the crash and today was his funeral.

The Laurel Valley residents had come together to honour a man they had all loved. Meg sat in the second row, letting the music and words flow over her. Her mother pressed a fresh hankie into her hand, replacing the tear-soaked one in her lap.

The last two weeks had felt surreal. Sure, she'd been back at work and she'd competently dealt with the usual issues, but her mind seemed stuck on the mountain.

From the moment the search and rescue team had arrived and put Meg on one horse with a bushman and Will on another, she'd lost contact with him. They hadn't spoken again.

The rescue party had brought them to the Mt Hume resort where her mother and brothers had been anxiously waiting for her. In the mêlée of hugs, she'd looked up to see Will getting into a luxury four-wheel-drive with a well-dressed older couple she assumed were his parents, his father a frail version of Will, his mother slim with ash-blonde hair.

And that had been the last she'd seen of him. But he had filled her thoughts both day and night. For two weeks she'd relived every conversation, every laugh and every sigh. And she'd replayed his kiss over and over—the pressure of his lips against hers, the surge of longing that had swept into every crevice of her body when she'd tasted him, the feeling of loss when he'd pulled away.

She'd spent hours imagining conversations with him should they ever meet again and how she would greet him if they did.

The organ music swelled and the pallbearers, Tom's sons and members of the footy team he coached, lifted the coffin high onto their shoulders and carried it down the aisle. Slowly the crowd filed from the church and Meg took a moment to say a few words to Tom's wife before heading out into the sunshine.

Meg turned to walk toward the hall where the women of Laurelton had prepared the wake. She knew the drill… standing around drinking tea, balancing a plate of sponge cake and sandwiches and making polite conversation. But her heart wasn't in it. People would ask about the crash and she didn't want to have to tell her story again. This was time to remember Tom.

Her mother's voice broke into her thoughts. 'Sheryl Jettison's offered to drive me home, so I'll see you later this afternoon.'

'Are you sure?'

Her mother nodded at her quizzical look. 'Go back to work. You're on call, so people will understand.'

'Thanks, Mum.' She cut back across the church lawn, the quickest way to get back to the bush nursing centre.

'Meg.'

Her breath caught in her throat. She'd know that deep, sensual voice anywhere. She turned slowly, wanting it so much to be Will but scared

she was superimposing his voice onto someone
else's. She didn't want to deal with the disappointment if she was wrong.

Will stood in front of her, his black designer
suit tailored to outline his broad shoulders and
long legs. In casual clothes he'd looked gorgeous
in a crumpled sort of way. In a suit he was strik-
ingly handsome, a forceful statement of a man
in charge.

'You came to the funeral.' *Well, duh, he's
standing right in front of you.* So much for the
conversations she'd practised in her head.

'I did.' He moved toward her. 'How are you?'
He spoke quietly. 'How's your ankle?'

She tried not to sound breathless. 'Fine. And
you, and your ribs?'

'Fine.' A subtle ripple of tension wove across
his shoulders.

Tension that she recognised all too well.
'Actually, Will, I'm not that fine. I'm not sleeping
at all.' The truth rushed out after two weeks of
putting on a brave front to her family and friends.

He gave her a wry smile. 'Me neither. Do you
keep replaying the crash in your head?'

'Yes.' It was a relief to tell him.

'Do you want to...?' Their words collided, spilling over each other.

Meg laughed and looked into his face. 'Go somewhere and talk? I'd love to.'

He gently took her arm and steered her toward his car.

The gentle pressure of his fingers sent delicious shivers of sensation along every nerve and every vein until she tingled all over.

He opened the door for her, his eyes crinkling in a smile as he released her arm and handed her up onto the running board of the vehicle.

She climbed into his four-wheel-drive expecting the luxurious smell of leather. Fabric seats greeted her and as she sat down she noticed a saddle on the back seat and a suitcase in the very back. A man on the move? She wondered where he'd come from and where he was going.

Will sat down next to her and started the engine. 'Where's the best coffee?'

She bit her lip. 'Technically I should be at the wake, so I really can't be seen in public having coffee. But I'm on call, so come back to the nursing centre and I can make you an espresso, a lattè or a cappuccino.'

He raised his brows. 'Café society *à la* Laurelton?'

'Hey, the Italians came and started the tobacco industry here. We know our coffee.' She smiled. 'Any more cheek and you'll wear it rather than drink it.'

He grinned his trademark smile, his even teeth looking very white against his tanned face. 'Fair enough. So direct me to the centre.'

Two minutes later she ushered him into the kitchen of the clinic and started to froth milk for two cappuccinos. 'Did you take your ski trip after the crash?'

'I stayed on the mountain for a few days. Probably not the best idea, but I thought I would still try and work on Jason Peters to donate money to my current project.'

She wondered if he was being deliberately vague about his job. 'How did you go?'

'I tried to ski but the whole idea of being social just drained me. I found myself listening to con- versations about the stock market, about the latest football player trading controversy and I thought, *Why am I here?*'

Complete understanding wound through her. 'I know exactly what you mean. I thought after a near-death experience you're supposed to gain pleasure from everyday things, but I get so frustrated. Two nights ago I had to walk out of a meeting before I exploded. The discussion was all about what colour the serviettes should be at the council dinner. I felt like saying, "What does it matter? Just pick a colour."'

He nodded, empathy and comprehension radiating from him. 'Then I went to Queensland to my parents' beach house. Bad idea. My usually non-maternal mother turned all motherly on me. Dad just wanted to talk work.'

'Is your dad a doctor, too?'

He shook his head. 'No, I'm the only member of the family in medicine.'

She tried to match up his words, none of them making a lot of sense. 'Your dad's not a doctor but he can talk medicine to you?'

'Right now I'm not working at the coalface, I'm more in the admin side of things.'

'Oh, is your dad on the hospital board?' Getting information out of Will was like pulling teeth. 'Sorry, I'm a bit confused how you can talk work when your dad's not a doctor.' She sat down opposite him, and slid his mug of cappuccino across the table.

Her eyes zeroed in on his hands as he wrapped them around the mug. Long fingers that had worked so hard trying to save Tom. Fingers that had warmed her skin and created such confusion and longing inside her with their touch that she could no longer sleep at night for thinking about them.

He sighed. 'It's complicated.'

She raised her brows. 'Try me.'

His expression flickered with indecision.

A jab of pain struck deep inside her. He didn't want to tell her. She saw the doubt on his face. He thought she might sledge him and who could blame him? He didn't trust her after her appalling behaviour in the snow cave.

She tried to breathe in against a constricted chest. In a way they'd shared so much on that mountain— life and death, survival and endurance. They shared a very close bond from that experience. She could sense that, drew comfort from it.

And yet there was a huge yawning chasm between them. A trench she had dug based on a false belief. And now it looked like that gap could not be breached.

The pain intensified and wrapped around her heart.

Will tried to marshal his thoughts, pondering if there was a succinct way to explain how his father's illness and family responsibilities had propelled his career in an unexpected direction. He ran his hand through his hair. Nope, there was no quick way to explain it. An outsider wouldn't be able to fathom how the Cameron clan worked.

But thinking clearly when Meg's clear blue gaze was focused on him wasn't easy. Her wide smile distracted him. The cute little frown lines between her brows that appeared when she concentrated distracted him. The way her breasts pressed together when she leaned forward to listen distracted him. And her slightly parted lips, whose taste he recalled so vividly, forced every thought from his brain.

Hell, he'd been completely distracted by her from the moment he'd met her. For two weeks she'd taken up residence in his brain. He'd be reading a book, only to discover he had no idea of what he'd just read because the thought of his hands tangling in her chaotic curls had sidelined him. The recollection of his lips tasting hers was seared into his memory and seemed to be on permanent replay. And he couldn't sleep at night because he missed the warmth of her body against his.

He'd come to Tom's funeral hoping to get closure on the whole crash experience. His plan was to spend the afternoon with Meg and then head back to Melbourne. An hour with Meg would tie up loose ends and put an end to this feeling of restlessness. After all, work, no matter what the job, had always been his focus, and there was no reason for that to change. One chance meeting with a woman would not affect that. Work was waiting and it was time to restart his life.

Meg suddenly pushed her chair back and stood

up, the feet of her chair scraping loudly against the linoleum floor. 'Would you like me to show you the clinic?'

He pushed away the feeling of disappointment that sneaked in at her businesslike expression. 'That would be great.' He stood and followed her. 'So how does the system work here?' Will looked around at the bush nursing centre, which he guessed had once been a busy hospital in days gone by.

'We lost our status as a hospital a few years ago, along with a lot of other bush nursing hospitals. Our last full-time doctor retired five years ago and we haven't been able to attract one since.

'We have a fully stocked clinic, though, and doctors rotate through here out of Winston. Occasionally we get a doctor who wants to ski and trades off some time in the clinic. Unfortunately, the Mt Hume resort clinic offers better conditions so just lately we're down to one half-day doctor session. I'm the nurse practitioner who is "it" for the rest of the time. I run the maternal and child health clinic, the well-women's clinic and I'm on call for emergency triage.' She spoke matter-of-factly, as if this was nothing out of the ordinary.

'But that's appalling. Laurelton's a reasonable-sized town, surely it deserves some hospital beds.' He experienced a fizz of outrage. 'And when do you get a day off?'

She smiled at him as if he were a child stamping his foot. 'I have a weekend reliever. As for deserving hospital beds, tell that to the number-crunching bureaucrats. Someone in a tall tower in Melbourne thinks it's perfectly fine for the elderly or seriously ill person to have to travel forty-five minutes down the road to Winston hospital. Rural communities do it the tough way and people from the city have no real idea what it's like. They take their health care for granted.' Her eyes sparkled and her cheeks flushed pink. 'Shocks you, doesn't it?'

This must have been what she'd looked like the night in the snow cave when she'd talked so enthusiastically about Laurelton. Then he'd heard the passion in her voice, now he saw the fire and spirit on her face. It gave her a glow that sent his pulses racing.

He wanted to share with her what *he* cared about, what gave his life purpose. He opened his mouth to speak but the loud chime of the front doorbell cut off his words. Someone had arrived in need of Meg. He'd just lost his chance. The clock was ticking—it was time to go back to Melbourne.

They both turned and looked through the double glass doors of the clinic. A young woman was pacing back and forth, looking left and right, her actions restless and frantic.

'I'll get the door.'

'I should go.'

Their words crashed into each other as they both stood still, both knowing they should move.

Meg scanned his face and for one brief moment he thought he saw regret in her eyes, but then the shutters came down and her professional look was back. 'Could you possibly stay another half an hour just in case I need you?'

Just in case I need you. For a crazy moment his heart kicked up a notch.

She tilted her head toward the door. 'I've been worried about Brittany for a few weeks, she's been very agitated.'

She needs you as a doctor, you idiot. Common sense kicked in. *She doesn't need you. She doesn't need anyone. She is the most independent, self-reliant person you've ever met.*

This was unfamiliar territory. Usually he was ducking for cover, avoiding women who stalked him in social situations, hunting him for his family name, intent on trapping him for his wealth. This time he didn't need to duck—in fact, he wanted to stand tall, be noticed and needed.

But he doubted he'd be needed, she was a competent nurse practitioner, but an offer to extend his time in her company was on the table and he'd take it. 'Sure. Happy to stay.'

He shushed the niggling voice that told him this was a bad decision.

She didn't want him to leave. Not yet, when they'd hardly had time to talk. Meg knew he wouldn't have stayed for her sake but he was a caring doctor. She doubted he would walk away from a patient.

She gave him a grateful smile and together

they walked up to the door. She'd been asking Brittany Chambers to drop into the clinic for weeks and now Brittany was here, she was worried how the eighteen-year-old would react. Meg pasted a smile on her face, pushed open the door and stepped outside. 'Hello, Brittany.'

The young woman turned and looked at Meg and then at Will, her pupils large black discs. Her gaze snapped back to Meg.

'Brittany, this is Dr Cameron, who's visiting from Melbourne.'

The young woman stopped pacing and looked straight at Will. 'Are you a psychiatrist? 'Cos I think I'm going crazy.'

Will smiled at Brittany and opened the door to usher her inside. 'I'm not a psychiatrist but I come from a pretty crazy family so that might help.'

Brittany laughed and some of her tension dissipated as she walked inside.

Will raised his brows at Meg and gave her a grin as if to say, Step one down, nine to go.

Meg let out a long, slow breath. With a smile and a quip, Will had just managed to engage a very prickly patient. On the way to the treatment room she pulled Brittany's history from medical records.

Walking into the room, she found Will leaning casually against the wall, while an overly thin Brittany paced. No white-coat syndrome here, no doctor behind a desk.

'At first I loved not being able to sleep, I got so much done. I could party all night and still make it to lectures in the morning.' Brittany's words rushed out.

'How is your concentration?'

Meg noticed Will kept his voice light and conversational and Brittany responded to it, giving him more information than she'd been prepared to give anyone else of late.

'At first it was fine but now I can't finish my assignments. I sit down to write and my attention keeps wandering.'

'Have you seen anyone about this?' Will's attention stayed completely focused on Brittany.

She shrugged. 'I went to the student clinic at uni but the doctor there didn't seem that interested. He just wanted to put me on sleeping pills and I didn't feel comfortable doing that.'

Meg sat down on the desk, in keeping with the casual tone Will had set. 'How are things with your boyfriend, Michael?'

Brittany bit her lip and her voice quavered. 'Not good.' She took in a deep breath. 'He's wonderful but I find myself getting so frustrated with him. One minute I'm the happiest person in the world and the next I'm yelling and screaming at him.' She dropped onto a chair, her hand beating a rapid rhythm on her leg. 'I can't go on like this.'

Will pulled up a chair next to Brittany. 'I've got some hard questions to ask, Brittany. Are you up to answering them?'

Brittany met Meg's gaze, her expression asking for confirmation that this was the right thing to do, that this doctor would actually listen to her.

Meg nodded. She'd seen Will in action on the mountain and she trusted his clinical skills. With Will, Brittany had a chance of a correct diagnosis.

The young woman turned back to Will. 'OK, Doc, shoot.'

Will glanced at Meg for a moment, his face serious with concern, and then his gaze returned to Brittany. 'You're overly thin, Brittany. Mood swings and lack of concentration can be caused by not eating enough.'

Brittany rolled her eyes. 'I'm not anorexic. My friends all hate the way I can eat anything in front of me and never put on any weight.' She turned to Meg. 'Remember the smorgasbord at Lauren Tonti's wedding?'

Meg laughed. 'The tables almost collapsed from the weight of all that Italian food.'

'I had three plates of main course and a serving of every one of the seven desserts.' She sighed. 'But I was hungry at the end of the wedding and Michael and I stopped at Nick's for a hamburger on the way home.'

'Did you ever feel bloated after eating?' Will rubbed his hand along his jaw.

Brittany looked a bit embarrassed. 'Um, no, but I got the squirts.'

'Diarrhoea?'

She nodded. 'It's been a bit of a problem lately.'

Meg started making mental notes—unable to sleep, massive appetite, mood swings. Could it be bipolar disorder?

Will shifted in his chair. 'Do you ever have times when all that restless energy drains from you?'

Brittany's eyes lit up in recognition. 'Yes, how did you know? Some days I bound out of bed and other days I just can't get up and fatigue sticks to me like clingwrap.'

Will leaned forward slightly. 'How long does that fatigue last for?'

Brittany thought for a moment. 'Maybe about a day or so and then I'm fine again, but it makes planning hard 'cos I don't know if that day is going to be a bad day or not.'

'Tell me about a bad day,' Will's soft tone encouraged.

Brittany's expression of gratitude streaked across her face. Someone was truly listening. 'My heart pounds so hard it feels like it's going to bound right out of my chest. I love to exercise but lately just walking up a flight of stairs leaves me breathless.' She started to fan herself. 'And I get so hot even on cold days that I'm giving the antiperspirant a run for its money.'

She gave a brittle laugh. 'Mum's the one supposed to be going through menopause, not me.' She bit her lip. 'It's driving me crazy. I think I'm going crazy. Don't you?'

Will shook his head. 'No, I don't think you're going crazy. I think you have a medical condition and we're going to work out what it is.'

Meg flicked through Brittany's file while Will continued to interview their patient. The family history section was scant as Brittany's previous clinic visits had mostly been for contraception.

'Brittany, you've had these symptoms at uni but did they start on the farm?' Meg started to think about water supply on the farm.

'No, I only started to feel unwell at uni.'

Meg's mind started to race. 'Where are you living at uni?'

Brittany looked at her as if she had two heads. 'In halls of residence, but living there wouldn't be causing all this stuff.'

Will gave Meg a direct look and a thread of understanding wove between them, connecting them.

They were on the same wavelength. The feeling was indescribable and a flush of heat whizzed through Meg.

Will voiced Meg's next question. 'What sort of job are you doing to keep yourself in pin money?'

Brittany groaned. 'I'm cleaning. It's awful but the money is really good.'

Meg slid off the table. 'I suppose you're using a lot of disinfectants.'

'Of course. Mum taught me the only way to clean is to use a lot of Shine O Kleen. I go through litres of the stuff but I've got happy customers.'

Will shifted suddenly in his chair. 'Meg, do you have a bottle of that disinfectant here?'

'I'll go and look.' She walked over to the cleaning cupboard under the sink and rummaged until she found a bottle. She quickly scanned the contents listed on the side. 'It contains iodine.'

Will gave her a nod of thanks, a smile tugging at his lips.

She wanted to hug that smile to her but she knew it was just a smile from a colleague sharing the satisfaction of making a diagnosis. A colleague who would be driving back to Melbourne very soon. Her stolen half-hour with Will, which she'd shared with Brittany, was about to end. He would leave and this time he had no reason to return. The knowledge sat like a lead weight in her belly.

Now she only had memories. They would have to be enough.

Will stood up, all action and intent. His brain was on fire with the challenge of a tricky diagnosis. He loved the jigsaw of medicine, putting the pieces together and coming up with the diagnosis. The last half an hour had been more exciting than anything he'd done in the last six months of pen-pushing.

And then there was Meg. The gorgeous Meg. They'd just shared a mental place in space, coming to the diagnosis at the same moment. The exhilaration of that instant had zinged through him, bringing back to life feelings he hadn't realised he'd missed.

Together they'd pretty much nailed the diagnosis. Now he just had to confirm the history with the examination. 'Brittany, I need to examine you. Can you slip your shoes off as well?'

'Sure thing, Doc.' Brittany hopped up onto the examining table.

Will did a thorough examination of Brittany from top to toe, noting her slightly swollen eyes and rapid pulse.

Meg walked over just as he was examining Brittany's ankles.

'Coarse and reddened skin on the shins.' Meg ran her fingers lightly over Brittany's foot.

Will met her azure gaze and a shot of heat ripped through him. 'Well noted.' The words came out husky and formal. What the hell was wrong with him?

Brittany reached down to her ankle. 'Yeah, what's that about? I put cream on them every night and nothing fixes it.'

Will pulled Brittany into a sitting position and threw a blanket around her shoulders. 'Based on your symptoms, we think you have a condition called Graves's disease.'

Brittany gripped the blanket, her knuckles white. 'What's that? It sounds deadly.'

Will gave her a reassuring smile. 'It's not deadly. It was named after the doctor who discovered the condition, Robert Graves. It's when your thyroid goes haywire and secretes too much thyroxine into your blood supply. This is what has been causing the palpitations, the hot flushes and all your other symptoms. Your body is in a constant state of hyper-alert and it's exhausting you.'

'But why?'

Meg glanced at Will for a brief moment before resting her hand on Brittany's knee. 'Sometimes it runs in families and we can find that out by interviewing your mum and dad. In other instances the condition can be sparked off by environmental things. The cleaning product you have been using is very high in iodine.'

'So if I stop using that stuff I'll go back to being normal?' The disbelief in the girl's voice mirrored the expression on her face.

Will shook his head. 'It might not be that simple. First of all you need to have a blood test for a definitive diagnosis and then I'll start you on medication.'

Meg picked up a tourniquet. 'Brittany, I can take the blood now and have it couriered to Winston and we can have the results back in about three hours.'

The young woman nodded. 'So, Dr C., you're

going to be in Laurelton for a while, right, to help me get sorted?'

'Dr Cameron is only visiting Laurelton today, Brittany.' Meg briskly slid the tourniquet over Brittany's arm and didn't look at Will.

'Oh, but I don't want to see another doctor.' Brittany's look of disappointment speared Will.

Suddenly her face took on a coquettish look. 'You know, Laurelton is gorgeous at this time of year, Doc, a perfect place for a working holiday.'

Will was sorry to disappoint her but him staying in Laurelton wasn't an option. 'I agree it's a beautiful place but—'

Brittany's hands suddenly moved to her hips and her jaw jutted. 'Besides, Meg needs some help—surely you can see that.' Brittany's green eyes stared him down, unflinching.

A twinge of conscience caught him. Meg worked extremely hard and mostly on her own.

Brittany switched her gaze to Meg. 'You're always on the lookout for a doctor, aren't you, Meg?'

Confusion swept through Meg's eyes. 'Yes, Laurelton always needs a doctor but—'

'So what's the problem?' The logic of the young bore down on him. 'If you've got no plans, surely you can stay for a while?'

The thought he'd rejected out of hand a moment ago rolled around in his head. His parents had insisted he take a month off work to recover from the crash, and although he planned to return tomorrow, no one was expecting him. Perhaps he could stay in Laurelton for a bit and be a doctor again for a few weeks. Take the chance while he could before he had to return to Camerons, balance sheets and business plans.

Meg finally spoke, confusion replaced with a streak of calculation. 'Working here wouldn't be all bad. You could combine a few weeks' doctoring here with some schmoozing on the mountain for research money. You could give something back to Laurelton after all those years of skiing.' She tilted her head and raised her brows, challenging him.

Slow, banked heat burst into life inside him, the flames flicking along his veins. Two sets of eyes bored into him. They had him over a barrel. He'd look a right bastard if he walked away. He shrugged his shoulders. 'Yeah, I guess I could do that. I can give you three weeks.'

'Excellent.' Brittany whooped. 'Just as well I was here. You two are hopeless at organising anything.'

Meg's tinkling laugh washed over him.

Suddenly the reality of what he'd just committed himself to hit him straight in the chest. Working in Laurelton meant working with Meg. Seeing her every day, breathing in her scent and listening to her melodic voice. Doing all that and staying detached.

How the hell did he do that?

CHAPTER FIVE

MEG locked the clinic door and let the bunch of keys that hung from a bright lanyard around her neck drop back against her chest. It was hometime.

Funny how some sayings stayed with you from childhood. Didn't matter which job she was in, she always thought of the end of the day as hometime.

She reversed the car out of the driveway and headed down the main street, the Avenue of Honour. The bare plain trees showed all the signs of buds about to explode with bright green hopeful shoots. Spring was coming to Laurelton.

And so was Will.

Sometimes her mouth ran way ahead of her brain and this afternoon was no exception. Agreeing with Brittany and suggesting Will stay for a few weeks, what had she been thinking?

She tossed her head. She'd been thinking of her

patients. It had been a blessing he'd been in town today. It had saved Brittany a trip to Winston, a trip Meg wasn't certain she would have made after her last experience with a doctor.

All Laurelton residents deserved to have a doctor even if it was only for a few weeks.

That was what her job was all about. Looking after Laurelton.

Sure, you were thinking about your patients but you were thinking about yourself, too. The dreaded rational voice piped up.

She hated to admit it but she hadn't wanted Will to leave. Since the plane crash she'd been uneasy, on edge. From the moment she'd heard his voice today she'd relaxed.

She loved listening to him, hearing his melodic tones range over words, the sound of the grin in his voice when something amused him, the caring intonation he'd used with Brittany that afternoon.

When she was with him she experienced a kind of calm she hadn't known since before she'd met Graeme. It was as if Will understood her.

She grimaced at the thought, knowing it to be

way off track, an idea that only existed in her imagination. The reality was that in the snow cave she'd blown her chance to find out about him by jumping to conclusions. She still cringed when she thought about her behaviour.

So there was no shared understanding between them. And today had proved that when she'd tried to draw him out on his job and his father, and he'd gone quiet on her. All they had in common was the fact they'd shared a life-and-death situation. And now they shared the stress of the aftermath.

Really, they were only colleagues.

That was all it ever could be. They came from different worlds and had different expectations of life. A caring man like Will would want marriage and a family. She couldn't offer him that. Graeme had stolen that dream from her.

Will would turn up each day, run the clinic and then hang out with his mates on the mountain. She would only see him at work. Which was a good thing. It kept things organised and uncomplicated.

A few minutes later her car shuddered over the cattle grid, the familiar thump, thump, thump heralding she was home. She was looking forward to sitting on the couch and doing nothing. The bookings for the B&B had been solid most of the season but the weekend guests were not arriving until Saturday so she had a night off.

As she rounded the final bend of bush track, the large red corrugated-iron roof of the farmhouse, with its four brick chimneys, came into view. In traditional Australian design, the roof extended to create a large veranda that surrounded the house, essential for the hot high-country summers that always seemed so at odds with the winter snow.

She loved this house. Every groan of the floorboards, every squeak of the gate, and the family history that lived in its memories.

No cars were parked in the car park. Great—no last-minute guests. Her black Labrador, Jet, bounded over to her as she got out of the car, looked up at her with huge brown eyes, and immediately nuzzled her hand.

Unconditional love. She'd decided a long time ago that humans could learn a lot from dogs.

'Hi, girl, how's your day been? Dug any bones?'

Jet ran around her, eager to please but with one eye in the direction of the food bowl.

Meg laughed. 'You wouldn't be hungry, would you?' She jogged to the veranda, Jet by her side, and pulled open the fly-screen door. Dumping her large carryall next to the boot box, she grabbed the dog food out of the old fridge and emptied it into Jet's bowl. As she stood up, her head hit a coat and the smell of oiled japara stung her nostrils.

The walls of the 'mud-room' were lined with hooks. Waterproof jackets, backpacks, riding gear and hats all hung waiting to be grabbed as people walked out the back door. The old fly-wire door used to slam a hundred times a day when she'd been a kid.

It didn't slam quite so much anymore and guests used the front door. She suppressed a sigh. The house needed kids. In the school holidays her nieces and nephews would visit, but in between times it was too quiet.

She walked into the kitchen. Her mother sat at the end of the enormous scrubbed wooden table, reading the paper. Her elbow crutches leaned against her chair. She looked tired and drawn, older than her sixty-two years.

'Hi, Mum.' Meg headed over to the large porcelain sink and washed her hands, then dried them on the towel that hung under the bench.

Eleanor looked up and smiled. 'Hello, darling. I hear that Brittany finally came to see you. Lucky you had that doctor visiting at the time.' She closed the paper.

Meg swung around in surprise and looked her mother. 'I see the Laurelton bush telegraph is working well.'

Eleanor smiled, refusing to be diverted from the topic in hand. 'Where is he from?'

'Melbourne.' She had no idea why but she really didn't want to talk about Will to her mother.

'He was the doctor on the plane, wasn't he? Will Cameron?' She put her reading glasses on the table. 'Sheryl recognised him from the paper. It was good of him to come to Tom's funeral.'

Meg nodded. Will wasn't anything like the man she'd thought he was. Unlike Graeme, he genuinely cared for people. 'He'd flown with Tom for years.'

'Brittany and her mother were raving about him. He sounds delightful.' Her mother gave her a long look.

Meg recognised that look. It was the 'you need a man' look that her mother and half of Laurelton specialised in. A rush of self-preservation shot through her. Men meant pain. She was not going to put herself out there ever again to experience that sort of grief. She had the farm. She had her job. It had to be enough.

She walked over to the fridge. 'What's for dinner? I'm starving. I plan to eat and then blob on the couch and watch a happy movie with a happy ending.'

'Sorry, sweetheart, we've got a guest.'

Meg suppressed a sigh. The farm needed the income but tonight she had so wanted the house to be guest-free. The idea of the movie evaporated. She'd be making beds and getting the guests settled. 'I didn't see a car when I drove up.'

'No, you wouldn't have, it's a bit early.' Her mother's voice sounded brisk.

'I'll go and make up some beds, then.'

'No, do that later.' Her mother stood up and

grabbed her crutches. 'You go and get freshened up and I'll get dinner happening.' She shooed Meg away by pointing a crutch.

Slightly confused as to the unusual order of things but happy to have a shower, Meg laughed. 'OK, who am I to argue with the boss?' She recognised when her mother meant business and knew there was no point objecting.

Ten minutes later, feeling refreshed by the warm water and the loofah rub, she was about to dry her hair when she heard a staccato knock on the front door. Her room was closest to the door. 'I'll get it,' she called, to save her mother the long walk from the kitchen.

The dull thud of crutches ricocheted up the hall. 'That's fine, honey, you finish drying your hair. I'll get it.'

First she had been instructed to have a shower, now to dry her hair. What was going on here? 'Don't be silly, Mum, I'm right here.' She pulled open the front door. 'Welcome to Big Hill Fa—'

Holding a large suitcase, a laptop and a saddle, stood Will Cameron. Surprise raced across his face, which he quickly schooled into an impassive expression.

Her stomach flipped over as she struggled to regain her composure.

Eleanor moved past a stunned Meg. 'So you found us all right, Will? My directions were pretty straightforward. Wonderful, come on in.'

Realisation streaked through Meg. Her mother had just called Will by name. Her mother had known all along that Will was the guest and hadn't told her. Some time after Will had left the clinic, her mum, Brittany Chambers's mother and Sheryl Jettison had cooked up a plan. And she and Will were the main course.

Meg stood in front of him, fresh-faced and wholesome, dressed in jeans and an Arran jumper. Her curls, some damp and clinging to her face, others exploding into clusters as they dried, made her look about sixteen.

Sixteen and bewildered. Her shocked expression was hastily replaced by a tight smile.

He recognised that expression. He was sure his

face wore the same one. He forced his voice out against a dry throat.

'Eleanor, good to meet you.' He stepped into the hall. 'I didn't realise you were Meg's mother.'

'Oh, didn't Sheryl mention that? Come on in, don't stand in the doorway. Meg, show Will his room and I'll go and pour some drinks.' Eleanor bustled around them and then limped away down the hall, leaving him alone with Meg.

'I had no idea…' His words tumbled out, matching Meg's.

She laughed, her gorgeous, tinkling laugh. 'Neither did I. Follow me.'

He walked behind her, his gaze riveted to her cute backside so marvellously defined by tight jeans. All too soon Meg turned into a room.

'You can put your case over there and I'll take the saddle out to the tack room.' She looked at the pile of neatly folded linen on the top of the box at the end of the bed. 'I'll make up your bed for you while you have a drink.'

He didn't want this. He didn't want to be the guest and her the maid. He picked up the sheets. 'Let's do it now and have a drink together.'

She raised her brows. 'We don't ask our guests to make their own beds. That's why we have a four-star rating.'

He ignored her expression and flicked the sheet out toward her. As the sheet floated down to the bed he caught a smile twitching at the corners of her plump lips.

He had an overwhelming need to explain how he'd landed on her doorstep. *Why? Do you think she'll assume you're chasing her?* He squashed the voice. Women chased him, not the other way around, and he had no intention of reversing the trend.

'When I left the clinic, I went to the pub about accommodation. Sheryl Jettison told me this weekend is Ski Carnival and the town's booked solid.'

'I thought you'd stay on the mountain.' Meg sounded perplexed.

The Mt Hume road was notorious. 'It's a hell of a winding drive along that road to come into Laurelton every day for clinic.'

She bent down and deftly pulled the sheet into a taut hospital corner. 'I suppose it is.'

He pushed on, uncertain if he was really welcome or not. 'Anyway, Sheryl told me most of the bed and breakfasts were full as well, but she knew one that had a vacancy.' He pulled the sheet tight as he folded it back to make the top pleat. 'I didn't realise Big Hill Farm was your farm.'

He looked up into eyes as blue as a summer's day, eyes that were shuttered down, emotionless. 'No, well, you wouldn't.'

She wasn't giving anything away. He had no idea how she felt about him staying at her home and working with her during the day. This feeling of uncertainty was new to him. 'Are you OK with me staying here?'

'Sure.' The word came out firm and emotionless.

A sigh of relief went through him. He bent down to flick the crinkles out of the doona.

'We need your money, so you can stay.'

His hands paused on the cover, her words stinging like a wasp. Tension tore at his muscles, rigidity wound through him. Money. With women it always came down to money. He knew that, hell, it had been drummed into him by

Taylor. This was no different. People only ever wanted him for his money.

A pillow hit him in the head. Laugher surrounded him. Confusion pulled at every part of him.

'Don't look so serious, Will. You're giving the town your professional services while you're here. You get free accommodation.' She grinned at him. 'And with bed-making skills like that, we might even pay you.' *

She walked out of the room, still laughing.

He sat down hard on the bed. He had no idea what had just happened. Just when he thought he knew how the land lay, it suddenly tilted sideways. How was he going to survive three weeks of this?

Saturday dawned bright, sunny and not a cloud in sight. Meg didn't feel quite as bright as the morning sun. She'd spent a large part of the night tossing and turning, knowing that Will was sleeping across the hall.

Meg stoked the wood heater and adjusted the air entry. She could see the bottom of the wicker wood basket, reminding her she really must cut more wood.

She pulled out eggs and bacon and started to prepare breakfast. Her mother had avoided being alone with her last night so Meg hadn't been able to say to her, 'What were you thinking?' Although she knew *exactly* what her mother and her friends had been thinking when they had suggested Will stay at Big Hill Farm, their matchmaking never being very subtle.

She usually ignored their schemes, not that there were many as she'd rejected most of the Laurelton bachelors. Couple-hood was for other people. Not her. She would never trust her love to a man again. She'd lost too much the first time.

Last night at dinner, Will, of course, had been the perfect guest. Entertaining and witty around the big oak table, he'd charmed Eleanor with his manners and his innate style. He'd complimented her cooking effusively. What wasn't to like?

But working with him was going to be hard enough. Sharing her home with him would be almost impossible. He'd promised her three weeks in Laurelton. In the grand scheme of things three weeks was a blip on the radar of life. In twenty sleeps, life would go back to normal.

It was simply a matter of staying detached.

'Morning.'

The frying-pan Meg was holding clattered onto the table. Her mouth dried as she swallowed hard. Quivers of sensation raced across her skin, every nerve ending sent into delicious, sensory overload.

Will stood in the kitchen doorway, his biceps bulging as he held an armful of wood. He strode forward and let the wood roll down his arms into the basket. As he straightened, his damp T-shirt clung to his chest, outlining a solid pack of muscles. Perspiration, combined with vibrating energy, poured off him. A man at one with himself and his achievements.

Jet stood by his side, looking up at him adoringly as he rubbed his hand against her coat.

Traitor!

'Thought you could do with some wood.' He grinned at her, his cheeks creasing into now familiar lines. 'Jet gave me a hand, didn't you, girl?' He bent down and cupped his hands around the dog's face and then rubbed her ears.

Jet slobbered with delight.

Meg stopped breathing.

A flash of memory—his hands cupping her face in the snow, his lips touching her own, the taste of salt, sweat and cold, the sensation of fire and yearning, and the regret of it being over so quickly.

'Thanks for the wood.' She forced the words out, hearing the huskiness that clung to them.

His eyes darkened to forest green flecked with brown. 'It's my pleasure.'

How she didn't melt into a puddle of pounding desire at his feet was a miracle. She swallowed. *Focus on the everyday things.* Gripping the frying-pan, she lifted it back to the stove. 'Eggs for breakfast?'

'Great. I'll just grab a quick shower.'

She nodded as she watched him turn and walk toward the bathroom. She heard the water start. Heard the thump of the shower door closing. The image of Will, broad-shouldered, sculpted chest, tight— Enough! She banished the delicious image from her mind.

I am so not going there. Banging the frying-pan down onto the hotplate, she slapped the bacon into the pan and forced all her concentration on creating a breakfast out of bacon, eggs, tomatoes, asparagus and Cape-seed toast. He would eat breakfast and head up the mountain for the Ski Carnival festivities. Hopefully he'd stay for the fireworks and stay the night as well. She could have a day without every nerve ending being on full alert.

'That smells fantastic.' Will, now dressed in moleskins and a chambray shirt, slid in behind the table, looking for all the world as if he belonged in her kitchen.

He does not belong here. He belongs in Melbourne.

'Let's hope it lives up to its aroma.' She placed two plates on the table and poured coffee, the pungent smell enticingly good.

He glanced around. 'Where's Eleanor?'

'Having a sleep-in. By Saturday she's usually pretty wiped so I do the weekend breakfasts and she does the dinners.'

For a brief moment a slight frown creased his forehead and she was certain he was about to say something.

But he reached for the pepper grinder and concentrated on peppering his eggs. As he placed the grinder back on the table, he looked straight at her, his eyes full of expectation. 'So what's on today?'

Confusion swirled inside her. 'Um, I thought you'd be going to the Ski Carnival.'

'I'm planning to avoid that madhouse.'

'Oh.' She knew she sounded vacant but she'd thought he would be spending the day on the mountain. 'Well, what sort of thing are you after? You could go fly-fishing for trout.' *Anything that means you're not at home with me.*

'Crikey, that water would be freezing.' He scanned her face. 'No, I don't think fishing is the thing. I read in the brochure in my room that there are fully escorted horse rides.'

A prickle of unease ran through her. She didn't like where this was going. 'I suppose that could be an option but—'

'Excellent.' He speared his asparagus and raised his brows. 'You once accused me of never staying in Laurelton and only skiing on Mt Hume. I thought I should remedy that situation and have you take me on a horse ride in the snow.'

The vision of having a recovery day at home away from his tantalising presence vanished. The two of them would be out in the bush on horse-back. Alone. Staying detached was going to take a monumental effort, an effort she wasn't at all at convinced she was up to.

Meg rose up in the saddle as Crafty cantered along the snow-covered fire track. Mountain ash rose straight and tall to the sky, contrasting with the snow gums' gnarled and knotted trunks, white bark on brown, creating asymmetrical stripes.

The only breeze was the one created by the speed of her horse and she leant her head back to enjoy the sensation. She was one with her horse, rising and falling with each step. So enjoying the sound of horse's hooves crunching on crystal snow and the joy of being in her beloved bush.

Completely unnerved by the fact Will was on a horse only metres behind her.

He'd helped her saddle the horses. She was feeling completely betrayed by her animals. First Jet had fallen at his feet, which wasn't unex-pected for a Labrador, but Diesel, who usually greeted strangers with distain, had nuzzled him when he'd whispered in her ear.

Meg didn't blame her for that.

Will certainly knew his way around a horse. His saddle, although well polished, wasn't new. He'd obviously been riding for years and he'd proved that by capably fitting the bridle, buckling the saddle and adjusting the stirrups. All of this raised her curiosity about what life experiences had moulded him into the man he was.

She really wanted to know about his life. She knew four things—he'd skied all his life, he'd gone to an exclusive private school, he could ride a horse like he'd been raised on one, and even though he was a brilliant clinician he wasn't currently working with patients.

Once they'd reached the national park and her favourite trail, she'd let Will ride ahead. But watching his long straight torso rising from the saddle in perfect balance, his broad shoulders rippling with fluid movement as he and Diesel moved together, had all been too much.

She'd pushed her heels into Crafty's side and cantered past him. Away from the longing that had grown inside her and now ached whenever she was near him.

With enough distance between them she'd slowed to a trot and headed Crafty toward the lookout.

'Whoa, girl, nearly there.' She pulled back on her reins and Crafty started to walk as the track narrowed.

Will rode up beside her, his face alive with the exhilaration of the ride, his hazel eyes the colours of the snow gums. 'That was fantastic! I've never ridden in snow before.' He patted Diesel on the neck as they rode side by side. 'On a sunny day with no wind, the conditions are perfect.' His lips curved into a smile. 'It's almost hot.'

She wanted to sink into his smile. 'True, but come back in November when the park is a mass of silken daisies and this is the only place in the world to see them.'

He grinned and the edges of his eyes crinkled. 'I see you have your tour-guide hat on.' His gaze zeroed in on her face, his eyes willing hers to look back into his. 'So what should I be appreciating now?'

She couldn't mistake the huskiness in his voice. They were out in the snowy Australian alpine bush on horseback, on a still and sunny day. If this were a story in a book they'd be falling into each other's arms right about now.

But this was real life.

He was relaxed and on holidays. The last time she'd fallen for a man, he'd been relaxed and on holidays. And she'd been badly hurt.

Remember that.

Playing the tour guide was the key to getting through the day. Lots of talking. That would avoid the long, questioning looks and loaded silences. That would get her through this ride.

Will sighed as Meg moved Crafty slightly in front of Diesel, breaking the moment. Meg did that all the time. He'd flirt, she'd retreat. It had happened from the moment they'd first met. He knew she admired his skills as a doctor but she didn't seem to warm to him as a person. He knew he shouldn't flirt with her but when she looked at him with her intoxicating wide blue eyes he couldn't help it. The words just came out naturally.

And she prickled every time.

Hell! He'd had enough practice ignoring flirting from women who did almost anything to get his attention. Once he'd come home to find a half-naked woman sprawled across his bed; another time he'd opened his door to find a three-course meal had been delivered along with the dinner company, a woman who'd wanted to get to know him. He'd even been called out to discover there hadn't been a medical emergency at all but a woman alone in a spa, waiting for him.

He'd become expert at dodging and weaving and avoiding predatory women, perfectly comfortable in his role as the rejector. He'd had no experience of being the rejected one until now, and he hated to admit it, but the role wasn't enjoyable.

He couldn't get his head around his fascination for Meg. The women he knew wore designer clothes and were never seen without make-up. Last night, Meg with her hair snagged back in a rubber band, wearing faded and threadbare jeans, had been the sexiest thing he'd ever seen.

Today in jodhpurs the trend continued.

She intrigued him like no other woman ever had. If only he could hide up here with her, away from the world. Away from the responsibilities that tied him. ❦

Will followed Meg and broke through the trees. A flock of king parrots flew past, a blur of red and green. Meg stretched her arms out wide to indicate the 180-degree view.

The lower reaches of the mountains, almost blue due to the eucalypts, shimmered in the sunlight. Further up, the snow clung to the rugged granite outcrops, a combination of snow and quartz sparkling a dazzling white. Deep in the valley below, clear alpine water rushed over rocks, tickling trout.

'That's one hell of a view.' Will gazed doggedly outwards, wanting desperately to stare at Meg.

As she swung off her horse, he sneaked a peek as her jodhpurs moved over the curve of her behind. His palm itched.

'It's also a great place for lunch.' Looping the reins around a log, she gave Crafty a quick pat and turned to unbuckle her saddlebag. 'I've got

the food and the picnic rug is in your saddlebag.'
Her voice was brisk and businesslike.

He was being put in his place. He was the
tourist, she was the guide. 'Right you are.' He
dismounted and found the rug. With a quick flick
he spread it out in full sunlight, rubber side
down, and sat, his back resting against the tree,
enjoying the view. The view of Meg setting out
the picnic.

She sat down next to him, also leaning against
the tree but with a clear handspan distance
between them. As if she was determined not to
have any accidental touching.

Pity.

She opened a wide-necked Thermos and the
aroma of nutmeg assailed his nostrils as she
poured the contents into a mug. 'Pumpkin soup.'

'Sounds great.' He accepted the proffered mug,
his fingers brushing hers at the handover. A shock
of sensation charged through him and went
straight to his groin. 'Thanks.'

She nibbled her bottom lip. 'No problem.'

But there was a problem. A great space seemed
to exist between them. He longed for the cama-

raderie they'd shared in the snow cave but it had vanished. The woman next to him seemed distant, detached and determined to stay that way.

His plan of spending the day together had backfired.

CHAPTER SIX

MEG ate her lunch, forcing herself to focus on everything around her except the fact she was sitting next to Will. He'd finished his lunch and now leant back, closing his eyes. He tilted his face toward the sun, his body relaxing, waves of tension draining from him as he stretched his long moleskin-clad legs out in front of him.

His legs ran parallel to hers. If she moved slightly, her leg would touch his. Her heat would mingle with his heat. Delicious sensation would whirl in her body, touching every dark corner.

She craved his touch.

But she didn't dare move her leg.

Nothing had changed. He still came from a different world. He was still only here on a holiday. He would leave Laurelton and go back to his life in Melbourne and she would stay. It was pointless to think, to imagine or to yearn. Reality meant they couldn't be together. She was damaged goods. He was only in Laurelton because he was needed as a doctor.

Laurelton was lucky to have him, even for a short time. She gazed at him, enjoying the view of his handsome face, the strength of his jaw, the line of stubble along his cheek.

Will's eyes opened and he smiled a long, bone-melting smile, his hazel eyes sparkling with flecks of peppermint green.

Horrified at being caught out staring at him, she tried to cover her actions with words, which tumbled from her mouth. 'I just wanted to say how excellent you were with Brittany yesterday. You put her at ease so quickly.'

'Thanks.' He grinned like a kid who'd just been praised.

Her heart gave an erratic beat at his boyish smile. *Keep talking about work.* 'Do you have a specific area of medicine you enjoy?'

'Paeds was my favourite rotation when I was a med student.' His eyes sparkled. 'I love kids, they never fail to make me laugh with their take on the world. I did my residency in paeds—lots of all-nighters with croup and asthma and terrified parents.'

She could picture him on the ward, the voice of reason, the epitome of calm, instilling a sense of security in the parents. Cuddling the kids.

A jagged pain ripped through her. He loved kids—of course, a generous man like Will would. She forced herself to comment, keeping her voice light. 'Yep, paediatrics isn't just treating the kids, is it?'

He nodded. 'More often than not, the kids' health is the easy bit. Dealing with the parents takes tact and diplomacy that they don't teach you in med school.'

She sat up, crossed her legs and leant forward, her interest piqued. 'So, after your residency, then what?'

'I made the move into paediatrics and started my specialisation.' A tightness appeared around his mouth, the familiar tension he wore was back.

'Oh. I thought you said you worked in administration?'

'I do.'

'OK, I'm totally confused. I've seen you in action twice. Your clinical skills are brilliant but you're currently not working in clinical medicine. How are you planning to qualify as a paediatrician if you're not working in the field?'

He sighed, a long, shuddering sigh.

Deep inside her something ached in sympathy.

'For the moment I've stepped out of clinical medicine.' His words sounded hollow.

'But why?'

He dragged in a deep breath, reached into the pocket of his jacket and pulled out a packet of lollies, balancing them in the palm of his hand.

Her confusion must have shown on her face. 'Lollies are the reason you're not working in the field?'

'Exactly.' The lines around his eyes seemed to deepen. 'Do you know who makes these?'

She picked up the familiar purple and green bag. She'd been buying this brand since she'd been a kid with an allowance burning a hole in her pocket. She read the fine print at the bottom of the bag. 'Camerons Confectionery.' Realisation dawned. '*You're* the Cameron in Camerons Confectionery, makers of fine lollies and liquorice since 1885?'

'Got it in one. My great-grandfather started the business and a Cameron has always been at the helm. My father is the current CEO.'

She sat stunned. Every kid in Australia and New Zealand knew about Camerons lollies—the delicious, gooey caramels, the liquorice allsorts you pulled apart piece by piece and the sherbet bombs that exploded in your mouth. The company was an institution and children and adults alike hummed the catchy jingle from the television commercials.

She met his gaze and saw the strain, saw a burden of something in his eyes. She sensed he'd both anticipated and assumed her reaction to the news. His shoulders had straightened, a muscle in his jaw spasmed and for one brief moment his hand fisted.

His almost aggressive posture confused her, and she suddenly realised he was waiting for her to say something. 'So you're the great-grandson of Mr Lollie Cameron. I don't get it. How does this stop you being a paediatrician? It's not like you became a dentist.' She giggled. 'Now, *that* would be a conflict of interest.'

His deep, rumbling laugh enveloped her. 'There's a thought. Perhaps I should have threatened the family with dentistry.' Some of the strain on his face faded.

A ripple of pleasure ran through her that she had lessened his tension but she wanted to know the whole story. 'Seriously, why does this affect you?'

He pushed his sunglasses up to the bridge of his patrician nose. 'I'm the first Cameron not to go into the family firm.'

'Wow, you really did rebel, didn't you? Forget drugs and rock and roll—you outclassed them all by becoming a doctor.'

His grin ignited thousands of sparks of desire deep inside her. *Listen to his story.*

'I've rebelled pretty much all my life, with varying degrees of success. My family is old money and it can stifle you if you let it. My parents did the traditional thing. Their marriage joined two well-connected families and together they are formidable economically, socially and politically.'

'Surely they liked each other a bit?' She pulled her knees up to her chin.

He shrugged. 'They have an affection for each other, I suppose that's grown over time. They believed their job was to run the company and have an heir. That's me, heir and only child. They stopped after me—their relationship is not what I would call true love.'

'Do you admire them?' Her curiosity peaked.

'I do. I admire their ethic of hard work, but I don't share the thrill they get from making money, wheeling and dealing. Somehow that gene skipped me.'

She thought of Graeme and his love of money at any cost. Suddenly she remembered how angry Will had become when she'd lumped him in with the other Penton party boys.

'So I'm guessing you didn't have that much in common with the lads at Penton. They probably thought you were a bit of a leftie.'

He laughed and his eyes sparkled, a kaleidoscope of brown and green. 'You're right—I didn't fit into that scene at all. I went through school with a bunch of firstborns who eagerly accepted the mantle of succession.'

She remembered her own childhood where money was tight. 'Still, school can't have been all bad.'

'No, it wasn't, and it gave me some great experiences. I love to sail, ride horses and visit other countries. I know I'm very fortunate to have had those experiences. I just would have chosen to do them with different people.' He drew a circle on the picnic rug with his finger. 'That's why I love medicine. I get to meet people from all walks of life, not just the privileged few.'

Dared she ask? 'But you must have some friends.' She nibbled her lip. 'A woman you got along with?'

His generous mouth straightened into a taut line.

For a moment she didn't think he would answer. She waited and held her ground, the question out there between them.

'For a time I believed there was, but it turned out Taylor found the Cameron money and name more attractive than me. In fact, she found another man more attractive altogether and thought I could support them both. Only problem was, I didn't know about the other bloke.' His voice betrayed his hurt.

A streak of protective jealousy shot through Meg, instantly mingling with irrational relief. He was single. She opened her mouth to speak but Will looked straight at her and kept talking.

'I'm not planning to marry.' The words hung between them. 'Money gets in the way of love, it never gives it a chance.' His voice sounded overly loud in the quiet bush.

A crazy jolt of pain shot through her. She gave herself a mental shake. Her reaction to his statement was ridiculous but it also scared her. She needed to change the subject.

A bright pink sticker on the lolly bag caught her eye. 'Five cents from each pack helps toward finding a cure for kids' cancer.' 'Has this got something to do with you?'

His face lit up. 'Yes. KKC is my baby. Did you know that around six hundred children died from cancer in Australia last year? Watching kids die from cancer has to be one of the hardest things I have ever done. You feel completely impotent and the deaths are so much harder because they are out of kilter with what we accept as the cycle of life.' He ran his hand through his hair.

Her heart turned over at his words. She couldn't have a child, but watching a child you loved die, she imagined, would be devastating.

'When I joined Camerons I needed to do something that kept me in touch with medicine. As the Cameron fortune is pretty substantial I set up a philanthropic trust called Kill Kids' Cancer. It's going really well and we've already donated a million dollars to cancer research, as well as improving hospital facilities. I love being involved in something like that.'

Relief flooded her. She now knew for certain he wasn't anything like the rich, self-centred Graeme. 'That's a fantastic thing to have done, but why have you left medicine to join Camerons?'

He gave a long, shuddering sigh. 'Dad's been pretty sick. He's recovering from a kidney transplant and while he's not physically able to work I've taken over the day-to-day running of the business.'

Sadness for him and his family streaked through her, mixed with bewilderment. 'I'm sorry your dad is so sick but why are you being asked to run the family business when your skills lie in medicine?' Meg studied Will's face, looking for subtle clues. There had to be more to this story.

'Camerons is a private company and Dad's illness was so sudden that there was no one trained to do his job. Certain business secrets need to be kept in-house so not just anyone could be hired. Any hint of Dad's illness gives take-over opportunities so I needed to step in until Dad returns or someone else can be groomed to take over.'

'But you've just finished telling me you don't want the sort of life your parents have.'

'I don't, but at this time I need to do this.' The finality in his voice said, Don't push me. For a moment his eyes flickered with an unreadable emotion and then the shutters snapped down. 'It's working well.'

'Really?'

'Absolutely.'

Something didn't ring true here. 'So you've given up your plans to qualify as a paediatrician?'

'No, they're just on hold for the moment. It's a short-term thing.' The tone of his voice developed an edge.

'How long have you been acting CEO?'

He hesitated. 'Six months.'

'Six months doesn't sound all that short-term to me and won't you run into problems with the medical board if you're out of your specialist training area for too long?'

Will abruptly stood up, ending the conversation. The next minute a snowball pelted her.

'No fair.' She scrambled to her feet as a second snowball hit her in the back.

The sun had made the snow sticky and the balls were easy to make. She hastily rolled some ammo. She threw three and missed by a mile.

He stood tall and dark, his streaks of blond hair giving him the look of a surfer. With his hands on his hips, legs apart and a traitorous smile clinging to his lips, he teased her. 'Can't you do better than that?'

It was a challenge she couldn't resist. She ran toward him.

He dodged sideways, but not before he curved a snowball to spin, splat, onto her arm.

She hurled two back. One fell short. The other hit him in the back. 'Gotcha.'

He paused for a moment and launched four more balls at her. A huge smile split his face, exposing dimples she'd never seen before.

Her skin tingled but not from the cold.

She dodged and weaved, chasing him down, closing the gap between them. A snowball hit her in the neck, icy crystals snaking down her collar. She squealed as the cold snow hit her hot skin.

Will's laugh had a wicked timbre.

'Right, you've had it.' She lunged at his back, her arms grabbing his shoulders, and she wrapped her legs around his waist, just like she'd done to her brothers when she'd been a kid. Hanging on with one hand, she shoved snow down his back.

'Arrgh!' He swung around as the freezing snow made contact with his shoulders.

His sudden movement loosened her grip and

she started to slip, pulling him down with her, a tangle of arms and legs.

She was laughing so much she could hardly breathe as she hit the snowy ground. ❧

Will landed on top of her, laughing equally hard, his legs lying along the length of hers. He propped himself up on his elbows. 'You OK?'

She nodded, unable to speak as delicious laughter unlike any she'd known in a long time bubbled out of her.

'Good.' The word came out deep and hoarse. His head was close to hers, his breath caressing her cheek, his eyes now the colour of a dark forest snagging her own line of vision.

Her laughter faded, replaced by thundering desire.

His lips hovered close to hers, tempting her with their memory of a soft yet firm touch that flamed her woman's heat. She wanted to have that experience again. Wanted to taste him, touch him, hold him.

Just one more time.

All rational thought fled. She pulled his head down to hers and very slowly ran her tongue along his bottom lip. He tasted of soup and sweets, heat and lust.

A guttural groan sounded in his throat. His lips took charge, pressing down on hers, sending shafts of delicious sensation deep inside her. His tongue trailed across her closed mouth, enticing her to open, insisting on entry.

She didn't need to be enticed. She wanted this so much. She welcomed him, drew him in, needing him. Needing to know she could be desired again, that as a woman she still had appeal.

Their tongues melded in a dance of lust and longing. His mouth played over hers, sometimes hard and demanding, often gentle and tender.

She didn't know which she liked best, but she took it all and wanted more.

His attention switched from her mouth. While he trailed sweet kisses with dangerous intentions down her cheek and across her jaw, his hands tangled in her hair. Heat surged from his fingers into her scalp, creating an electricity that connected them, crossing back between them.

She caressed his face. Stubble scraped on her fingertips as she outlined his cheeks, memorising the feel of him. She breathed in deeply, inhaling his scent of citrus and wood, essence of Will.

His tongue found her ear and white lights exploded in her head. His hand sought a gap in her jacket studs and his thumb caressed her already pointed nipples through her shirt. Heat pooled deep inside her, tingling need making her moist.

She arched against him, needing to feel him, wanting him to lie against her, but layers of clothing and jackets got in the way. Frustration surged inside her and a strangled moan of exasperation escaped.

Will immediately drew back, his eyes glazed, his face contrite. 'Sorry. I wasn't thinking. Of course, this isn't the time or place.' He moved abruptly and stood up, pulling her to her feet. The moment she was standing he dropped her hand.

His gaze cleared, his eyes blank of all emotion. 'I'll check the horses' hooves for ice build-up.' The words shot out rough and harsh. He brushed snow off his moleskins. 'We should head back.'

She watched him go, crying inside, devastation pounding her. She'd been rejected. No confusion there at all. There would never be a time or a place. For a few brief moments she'd savoured the wonder of being desired but it was all an illusion. He didn't want any involvement with her and that was why he was walking away.

Diesel carried him back to the farm at a cracking pace. Will welcomed the complete concentration required to keep his seat as the horse cantered, the hooves eerily silent on the soft snow. The occasional dull thud of snow falling from the trees was the only sound to break the silence of the winter bush.

That seemed to go pretty well. Yeah, right. Kissing Meg again had to be one of his more stupid ideas. Hell, it had only been two hours ago that he'd decided he shouldn't flirt with her. So what had he done? Kissed her so hard his head had spun. Was still spinning fifteen minutes later.

What was it about this woman that completely undid him? Once before he'd fallen for a woman. Taylor. But he'd been young and naïve. When it had become obvious Taylor had only wanted him for his money, he'd shut a part of himself down and avoided relationships. If marriage were a business merger, he'd have no part of it.

But his reaction to Meg was all-consuming and it terrified him. It made his feelings for Taylor look innocent. Somehow during the conversation she'd managed to find out more about him than he'd planned to reveal. But it had felt so good, telling her about KKC, right up until the point she'd started asking the hard questions. The ones that had no answers.

Every woman he had ever met paled into insignificance when compared with Meg. Yet he had no real idea what he wanted, except his need to hold her close.

When they'd fallen in the snow, kissing her had been the natural thing to do. It had felt so right.

His arms ached from wanting her back in them. He could smell her wild-rose scent on his jacket, the perfect scent for a woman who loved the outdoors. He could still taste her sweetness and picture her eyes darkening with what he'd thought to be a desire to match his own.

But the sound she'd made when he'd touched her breasts had been like a bucket of cold water, bringing him back to reality with a jolt. She didn't want him. She wasn't playing hard to get. She just wasn't playing, period. And he hated it.

The memory of her hands on his face rocked through him. She'd pulled his head down to her lips. At the start of the kiss she'd been a willing participant. So what had happened? What was going on?

He suddenly realised that although he knew quite a lot about Meg, in other ways he knew nothing. At times she'd talked passionately about the farm, Laurelton and her job, but she'd ever mentioned a man in her life. A woman as gorgeous as Meg surely wouldn't be alone. Was that it? Could that explain her pulling back?

He didn't know but he was determined to find out.

CHAPTER SEVEN

MEG quickly tidied up the clinic's reception area. The Latham twins had demolished the toy box earlier in the morning during a busy session. Will was currently taking a break in the kitchen, which was why she was in Reception, avoiding him.

Her days had evolved into a pattern. She left early each morning to avoid Will at breakfast. Even though she was with him all day at work, there was something about sitting around the large farm table with him, sharing the paper and laughing over the comics, that caused her pain, and reinforced a general feeling of loss.

Every emotion she'd experienced around her diagnosis of infertility three years ago had come roaring back like a wall of water blasting through a flooded canyon. Part of her had sometimes wondered if she might meet a man who didn't want his own child. But the one man who was turning her world upside down loved kids, as she'd known he would. He'd chosen paediatrics as his specialisation. No one went into paediatrics if they didn't want to have their own children.

So she'd created a few survival tactics to help her get through the three weeks with Will. The end of the first week was looming and so far, so good. He ran his clinics and she ran hers. They met for a working lunch, a case conference, discussing the patients they had seen and signing off on treatment plans. Then he headed off for his house calls and she did her health education sessions.

At night she had the safety valve of her mother, who always ate with them. On the couple of occasions Eleanor had tried to make herself scarce, Meg had insisted on her joining in a card game or watching a movie with them. She'd almost eliminated non-work time alone with Will.

But it was exhausting. He had such an effect on her that she knew exactly where he was in a room. She could feel his gaze on her almost all day. She found herself breathing more deeply when he stood next to her so she could enjoy the scent of his fruity aftershave, and she had to force herself not to openly stare at him. When he'd worn his reef-green striped oxford shirt, his eyes had become almost magnetic, the shirt's colour deepening their intensity.

He wore clothes with the style of someone who knew quality and cut. But then again, he'd probably been dressed like that since birth. Although he enjoyed the finer things of life, she got the impression his wealth didn't sit easily with him. He'd deliberately closed the conversation about his work and family the other day, piquing her curiosity.

Her mobile rang. Meg listened to Sally Boon's worried voice. She tried to reassure her. 'Bring Brodie in now and I'll grab Dr Cameron so we're both ready when you arrive.' She punched the 'off' button and headed down the corridor to find Will, trying to stomp on the image of her hands grabbing Will's shirt, his shoulders, his body…

She found him standing with his hands deep in the pockets of his khaki pants, staring out the window at the snowy peak of Mt Hume.

She rested her hand on the doorframe and took

in his broad shoulders and straight back, smiling at the way his hair curled when it hit his collar. Admiring him from a distance when she so desperately wanted to admire him from up close. But there was no point thinking like that.

'Will.'

He turned and smiled. The corners of his eyes crinkled, his irises sparkled, his cheeks creased in familiar lines and laughter played around his mouth.

His smile melted everything inside her, and desire hummed along every nerve ending. She gripped the doorframe. •

His gaze lazily traversed her body and then locked with her eyes. 'The view's amazing.'

Her mouth went dry. Her mind went blank. In a haze of lust her brain vaguely registered he wasn't talking about the mountain. She struggled to focus. 'We've got a patient.'

His stance changed immediately. The professional was back. 'Who is it?'

'Sally Boon, first-time mum and a crying baby.'

He tilted his head to the side. 'I thought you'd be happy to handle that on your own.'

'Usually I am, but there was something about Sally's voice that's got me worried.'

He walked toward her and grinned. 'I always listen to nurses' intuition—they're rarely wrong. I'll hang back and let you do your maternal and child health stuff but I'm here if you need me. We're a team.'

A team. He considered her part of a team. A little thrill tripped through her as she relived his words. She wasn't used to being part of a team. For a long time she'd battled pretty much solo to keep a form of health care going for Laurelton. Having Will there meant so much to the locals.

And so much to you. She refused to think about that.

She found her voice. 'Thanks.'

'You're welcome.' The deepness of his voice vibrated around her.

Heat and longing pulsed through her and she forced herself to turn away from his gaze and walk down the corridor. *You're a nurse, he's a doctor, this is work.* She ran the words over and over in her head.

The front door swung open and a dishevelled

young woman stumbled through. She carried a large nappy bag on one shoulder, clutched a baby in her other arm, and a bunny rug trailed along the ground.

'Meg, he won't stop crying.' Exhaustion and despair wove though the woman's voice.

Meg put her arms out to take the baby, who was currently quiet, his large dark eyes taking in his new surroundings. 'So, what's up, Brodie?' She deftly lifted the baby high onto her shoulder, and nuzzled his head with her cheek.

Will made an odd sound, almost a moan, followed by a cough.

Surprise shot through Meg. Was he waiting for an introduction? Usually he introduced himself. Confused, she swung toward him. 'Sally, I'd like you to meet Dr Will Cameron, who's working in Laurelton for a few weeks.'

Will shook the woman's hand. 'Pleased to meet you, Sally. Meg says your little fellow's been crying a lot.'

Sally followed them down to the treatment room, talking all the time. 'He's not feeding very well either, and I have to wake him up.

When he feeds he sicks up and he seems sort of floppy.'

Meg frowned. Floppy didn't sound good. 'Does he really vomit out a stream or is it more of a posset?' She laid Brodie on the examination table and stripped him down to his nappy to examine him.

'He doesn't always sick up, but today he has been.'

Meg put her hand on his scalp, her fingers examining the fontanelle. Her fingers dipped. A concave fontanelle meant dehydration. 'He feels a bit warm so let's take his temperature.' She kept her voice upbeat. No need to worry Sally just yet but she glanced over at Will, her eyes seeking his.

His direct look of support focused her. He was here to help if there was more to this than an unsettled newborn.

She felt his arm brush hers as he moved in next to her and a fire of sensation ran up her arm.

'Here's the ear thermometer.' His deep voice made her heart skip.

'Thanks.' She forced a briskness into her voice that she didn't feel.

The thermometer beeped. 'Thirty-nine degrees Celsius.' That was too hot. She peered in close and examined Brodie's face. 'Sally, what happened to his eye?'

'I guess he must have scratched himself. I didn't realise babies' nails could be so sharp.'

It might be an abrasion but it worried her.

She took down his nappy and the baby started to cry. A high-pitched cry. A lusty cry was normal. A cry like this was rarely good news. Picking up the stethoscope, she stretched her hand out toward Will.

A wave of silent communication passed between them. His hazel eyes darkened with unease and he caught her concern as she tilted her head slightly toward Brodie's chest.

Sternal retraction. The baby's chest sank inward as he struggled to breathe.

She handed Will the stethoscope and turned to Sally.

'Dr Cameron's going to listen to Brodie's chest.'

'Just warm your hands up first, Doc.' Sally managed to laugh, seeming to miss the implication of the transfer of care.

Will's brows moved together in concentration as he listened to the baby's air entry, moving the stethoscope carefully around the baby's chest, front and back.

She waited for him to pull the stethoscope out of his ears. 'Congestion?' She spoke quietly.

He nodded. 'Limited air entry. Could be pneumonia. I'll examine him thoroughly.'

She watched his meticulous approach to the examination as he gently palpated Brodie's abdomen. This was the trainee paediatrician in action. The doctor who should be doing this sort of work every day instead of being a philanthropic businessman.

His large yet gentle hand dwarfed the baby's tummy. A prickle of apprehension ran through her as she noticed him repeat his palpation of the liver.

Meg whispered the words that worried her. 'Is his liver enlarged?'

'Yes, it is.' His voice equalled hers in softness.

'Poor feeding, lung congestion, high fever, enlarged liver.' She looked at him questioningly. 'Could be a lot of things. What about his eye? I'm worried about that.'

She ran her hand over Brodie's head in a tender caress, but the ache she tried so hard to keep at bay when handling babies spasmed deep inside her.

Chlamydia meant she could never have a child of her own. She could only ever be a bystander. Graeme had stomped on her heart and trampled her dreams of a family of her own.

Will leaned in close, his thick chestnut hair gleaming under the examination light.

Brodie screamed, his little mouth opening wide.

A flash of dark red mucosal tissue caught Meg's eye. She grabbed the penlight and shone it into his mouth. 'Look, can you see that?'

Will waited for Brodie's next cry and peered into his mouth. He turned back and sought her eyes.

She could see his brain calculating, adding up the symptoms, diagnosing.

'You're thinking HSV, aren't you?'

She nodded. 'It looks like a herpes zoster vesicle and his eye would line up with that.' She pulled open a drawer and grabbed a small tongue depressor. She handed it to Will and held the light steady.

At the back of Brodie's throat they could see a cluster of cold-sore-like eruptions.

'What's wrong with him? Is it serious?' Sally's voice suddenly sounded small and terrified.

Meg exchanged a knowing glance with Will. She had to be the one to talk to Sally because she knew her best, but this would be one difficult and horrible conversation.

'Sally, we think Brodie has herpes.' Meg kept her voice neutral.

'Herpes?' A shocked look crossed her face. 'How would he have got herpes?'

'This is what we need to find out. The abrasion around Brodie's eye looks like a herpes blister caused by the herpes simplex virus.'

'But how could he have that?' Disbelief skated across her cheeks.

'There are a few ways. Has anyone cuddled him who has a cold sore?'

'No. No one.'

A wave of nausea at what she had to say next rolled through her. There was every chance this woman's world as she knew it was about to be tilted on its axis. Just like hers had been two years ago. 'Sally, have you ever had genital herpes?'

A look of pure disgust slashed the other

woman's face. 'No. No way. I've been faithful to Mark and him to me. How could you suggest such a thing?'

'Sally, I'm sorry to have to ask you and I'm not trying to imply anything, please, believe me. But I'm afraid to say that the most likely way a baby can get the condition is from its mother during delivery.'

'But I told you, I don't have it. I mean, you know when you have herpes, right? You have those blisters all over your...' She paused, her gaze dropping away from Meg's. 'I really resent you not believing me.'

'I believe that you believe you don't have it, Sally. We're just trying to work out a diagnosis for your very sick baby.' She tried to smile, to reassure Sally, but ended up biting her lip. 'Herpes doesn't always present as blisters. It can be burning and itching of your labia and vagina, redness and soreness. Has that happened to you?'

Sally started to shake her head and then stopped. Colour drained from her face, her eyes widened and she sat down hard on a chair. Her voice, barely audible, choked on the words.

'Mark went to the Philippines on an end-of-season footy trip. I was seven months pregnant and tired and…' Her voice trailed away.

Anguish at the woman's pain wound through Meg. She put her arm around Sally and looked over at Will, but he was busy with Brodie. What did you say to someone who'd just realised everything they'd believed in had just crumbled to dust?

Sally dropped her head into her hands and sobbed. 'After he came home I did have that burning and itching but I thought it was just pregnancy. Oh, God! How could he?'

A moment later her shoulders straightened and she stood, shrugging off Meg's touch. She raced across to Will, gasping at the sight of an oxygen mask on her baby's face. 'Will Brodie be all right?'

'He's extremely sick. I'm going to put in an IV and he'll need to be airlifted to the Royal Children's Hospital. He'll be nursed in Intensive Care and be given antiviral medication for three weeks.'

Sally gripped Will's arm. 'Will he be normal?'

Will's mouth tightened for a moment. 'At this point, I can't say how the disease will play out. His eyesight could be affected.' He put his hand over Sally's. 'All I can say is prepare yourself for a long struggle. Brodie is going to have to fight to beat this.'

Sally's stifled scream tore at Meg as she dialled the number of the neonatal emergency transfer team. While she organised the evacuation, she kept her arm around Sally, who was pale and shaky. Shock had set in.

As she finished the phone call, she grabbed normal saline and the smallest IV cannula she had. 'Sally, I have to help Dr Cameron put in the IV. You need to ring Mark and your mother because you're going on the helicopter to Melbourne with Brodie.'

Sally stared at her blankly.

Meg turned her toward the phone. 'Ring your mother, Sally. You need your mother.' She would need all the love and support she could get.

Will swabbed Brodie's tiny arm and with a touch of pure gentleness he slid the needle into the vein.

Meg placed a thin polyurethane dressing over the site then fashioned a small splint out of a tongue depressor to protect the area. The last thing they needed was the IV coming out.

She and Will worked wordlessly together and yet completely in unison, anticipating each other's needs. Not unlike on the mountain. She'd never worked with a doctor in this way before. Feeling like she was an equal partner in the situation.

Finally, half an hour later, the noise of the helicopter sounded overhead as it prepared to land in the car park of the pub across the road from the clinic. With a great sense of relief they transferred Brodie and Sally to the care of the emergency team. Meg ran away from the circling blades with Will close by, and watched the helicopter rise, bank and head west.

Meg breathed out slowly, glad Brodie was on his way to Melbourne. Trying to match Will's long stride, she joined him in the walk back to the clinic, snatching surreptitious glances at him.

His shirt, usually so crisp, was crumpled and had become untucked. His hair, which had been stylishly groomed earlier in the day, stood up in blond spikes where he'd tugged at it in an unconscious action of stress.

Her stomach flipped over. *Stop this and get serious.* Dragging in a breath, she nailed a reminder to her brain that Will had walked away from her the other day after kissing her senseless. She had to stomp on this attraction. It would just be a dead-end road of heartache. Like with Graeme. And there was no point thinking Graeme had been a one-off experience. Look at Sally. She'd married a man, trusted him completely and he'd put his son's life at risk.

Punching the clinic door open, her brewing anger exploded into a storm. 'What a jerk. How could he do that to her?'

Will followed. 'I gather you're talking about Sally's husband?' He opened the fridge in the clinic kitchen and poured them both a drink of water.

She accepted the proffered glass. 'Of course I am.'

'He was stupid. Selfish. But...' he heaved out a resigned sigh '...people make mistakes. I doubt he meant to make his son dangerously ill.'

Disbelief rushed in. 'Oh, so you're defending him, are you? Men have the right to cheat on their wives and then infect them with a sexually transmitted disease?'

Will raised his brows and looked at her as if she

was acting like a three-year-old. 'No, I'm not defending him. I'm just saying that he made a foolish mistake and didn't realise the consequences.'

She clenched her fist. 'Well, I think he's going to realise them now. He could lose his family.' Her voice rose. 'Men have to start thinking with their brains. Thoughtless actions like this scar, they damage, they ruin women's lives and…' She was horrified to find her throat had gone tight.

This wasn't happening. She'd dealt with what Graeme had done to her. She'd moved on with her life. She was independent, in control. She wouldn't fall apart. Not in front of Will.

But her chest wouldn't move in or out, wouldn't take in air. Her fingers tingled. Panic swamped her. Will's face started to swim.

She forced out the words she didn't want to say. 'Help me.'

Will saw the panic and fear in Meg's eyes. Damn it, she was hyperventilating and he had no idea why. He spun around. Where was a paper bag when you needed one? 'Hey, hey, it's OK.' He came around behind her, gently cupping his hands over her mouth and nose. 'Slow down, breathe in deeply.' He kept his voice low, wanting to break through her panic.

Slowly, as she breathed in her own carbon dioxide, her frightened grip on his hands lessened and her breathing became deeper, more regular. Her shoulders dropped and she relaxed against him. Her heat seeped into him. He'd missed that.

Her hands rested on his and she gently pulled them away from her face and turned toward him. The desolation in her azure eyes pierced him. What had caused her this sort of panic?

In a reflex action he drew her to him, cradling her against his chest, hugging her close. Keen to comfort, desperate to soothe away that haunted look. Panic attacks were common after trauma but they were usually linked with the event. Had seeing the helicopter brought the plane crash flooding back?

Her hair brushed his cheek; her powder-fresh scent enveloped him. He longed to plunge his face into her curls, explore her neck with his lips and fingers. Imprint her scent and flavour to memory.

But she needed the support of a friend, someone who'd experienced the same thing. Not a man driven wild with desire. He breathed in deeply.

He murmured against her ear. 'We've had a roller-coaster ride, you and I. Survived a plane crash, lost a dear friend and today we dealt with a pretty sick baby. It all adds up. Allow yourself to experience these emotions, it's nothing to be embarrassed about.'

She tensed in his arms and very slowly raised her head and looked at him. He saw a weary pain flicker in her eyes. Felt the sigh shudder though her body.

And suddenly he knew. 'This isn't about the plane crash, is it?'

He only just caught the slight side-to-side movement of her head before she stepped out of his arms. He saw a blank expression slide across her eyes and the control thud back into place.

'Sorry about all that. I don't know why it happened. I'll just go clean up the mess we made in the treatment room.'

He resisted the urge to haul her back against

him, cage her in his arms until she told him what was going on. For some reason he wanted to know. Since Taylor's duplicity, he'd walked away from anything that involved a real personal connection with a woman. But he and Meg had shared so much on the mountain, and working with her this last week had been amazing. She was in crisis and he wanted to help. He pulled out a chair. 'How about you sit down with me and talk about it?'

'No, really, I'm fine.'

He raised his brows. 'You couldn't breathe. What if that happened when you were treating a patient and you were alone, as you usually are?'

Her shoulders stiffened as she bristled at his words. 'It didn't happen, it has never happened and it won't happen.' Her words peppered him like buckshot.

He reached out and put his hand on her arm. 'Something happened today to really upset you.'

She looked away, unable to meet his gaze.

'I want to help, Meg.'

She turned back to face him. 'You can't.' The flat tone of her voice shocked him.

'I can if you let me. You don't want to risk your job, or your patients, I know you don't.'

She glared at him, her face tight with emotion. Pain intersected with sorrow and a reluctant acceptance of reality. 'That was low.' She clenched her fists.

He racked his brains, trying to work out the sequence of events. She'd been her usual competent and in-control self the whole time she'd been with Brodie. He quickly skated over his own feelings of being kicked in the solar plexus when Meg had nuzzled the baby close to her chest.

She'd been brilliant with Sally, able to draw her out, be empathetic and understanding. Which was no mean feat when a woman was dealing with the news of a desperately ill baby and an unfaithful husband.

He thought over the events of the past week but nothing stood out so he scanned back to the night in the snow cave. The conversation when she'd been so determined to cast him as the bad guy. Instead of really listening, he'd just gone into defence mode. What had she really said?

He remembered the bitterness in her voice and

the talk of Penton old boys. But she hadn't hyperventilated then, she'd just been angry.

What had happened today, just before she'd panicked? She'd been talking about the father of the baby. *Men...they ruin women's lives.* Had someone ruined hers?

'A man hurt you, didn't he?' The words hung between them. 'Talking about it will help, honest.' He smiled at her, wanting to convey his concern, knowing she normally responded to his smile. He hoped it would relax her. It was a long shot but he was fast running out of ideas and she looked ready to bolt.

The tension in her body, which had held her rigid, seemed to flow out and she abruptly sat down into the chair. 'I was briefly engaged.'

'An old Penton Grammar boy?'

Her gasp confirmed his suspicions.

'Yes. Graeme Stockward.'

He groaned inwardly. He knew of Stockward's reputation as a playboy.

'I was busy planning the wedding and he was busy planning not to be there. Turns out he thought it more of a holiday romance. He was occupied elsewhere, sleeping with every second woman he met. His parting gift to me was chlamydia.'

A white-hot rage flared inside Will. He wanted to punch Stockward so hard his perfect dental work would be shattered.

He put his hand out to cover hers.

She pulled her hand back, rejecting his touch. 'As you know, chlamydia can be hard to diagnose and I had no reason to suspect I had an STI. Graeme was always so attentive when we were together that I had no reason not to trust him.' She bit her lip. 'But three months after he left me I discovered his legacy. A raging infection and two blocked Fallopian tubes.'

Her loss stabbed at him. 'He's scum, a complete low-life.' The words seemed inadequate.

'I know that…now.' A weak smile struggled to form. 'And after I contacted his new girlfriend and we started a tree of contacts, I think he's out on his own.'

'Revenge is sweet?'

She shook her head. 'It wasn't revenge. I didn't want any other woman to go through what I had.' She folded her hands in her lap. 'Of course I had the full treatment of antibiotics and the infection's gone, but none of that changes the fact that I can't have children. I'm normally fine with it but watching Sally go through what I went through, I guess it tipped me over the edge.'

She ran her hands along her skirt, brushing away imaginary dust and specks, and then sat up a bit higher. 'Laurelton's health care is my job, as is the farm. We don't all need to be part of a couple. I've loads to keep me occupied and plenty of reasons to be happy. Don't you dare think about feeling sorry for me.'

Her look of fierce determination, mixed with permanent loss, lashed him. He knew her words were to convince herself as much as him that she was OK. Her drive, her will to make the best of each situation pulled at him. She didn't get anywhere near enough support in her job but she'd work herself into the ground before she'd give up.

'I wouldn't dare feel sorry for you.'

'Good.' She bit her lip.

Her action undid every intention he had of giving her the space she needed. He hauled her into his arms and crushed her against him, wanting to kiss her better, remove the pain in her life, banish the memory of Graeme Stockward for ever.

The incessant ring of the clinic phone echoed around them.

She pulled back from his arms, her sky-blue eyes large, her lips wet, her expression bewildered. Her voice trembled. 'We better get back to work.'

She spun away, her pain evident in her stance, and answered the phone.

Hell! He'd been dismissed. Again.

But this time he knew why.

Meg saw herself as dented and broken, unable to have a child, unable to offer the gift of life to a man. So she rejected any advances.

She needed the legacy of that bastard Stockward to be wiped away.

He couldn't give her back her fertility but he could give her back the knowledge that she was a vibrant, gorgeous woman who was amazingly sexy and desirable. Meg deserved to be romanced…a warm room, a large bed and a slow seduction.

A plan started to form in his head. The only sticking point would be convincing Meg.

CHAPTER EIGHT

OUTSIDE in the Laurelton spring sunshine, Will bit into one of Nick's hamburgers with the lot, enjoying the rush of childhood memories that came flooding back. His dad had spent his life making money but he'd occasionally dropped into father mode. Skiing holidays had been as close to father-and-son bonding as he'd ever got until the last six months. Illness had changed his father, brought out a softer side.

Being a temporary CEO for Camerons had given him an unexpected opportunity to really get to know his dad, and he'd loved their long talks ranging over all sorts of topics after the business side of things had been dealt with. Perhaps he should ring him and suggest he come up for a day of fly-fishing…

'Hey, Doc!' Brittany slipped into the moulded

plastic chair opposite Will and helped herself to a hot chip.

Will pushed the chips toward her and passed the tomato sauce. 'How are things, Brittany?'

The young woman had an air of relaxation about her that had been absent two weeks ago. 'I'm feeling great, Dr C., and I wanted to thank you.'

Satisfaction and pleasure welled inside him. 'Glad I could help.'

'You have no idea what it was like, Doc. I really thought I was going mad. But now I'm feeling well enough to head back to uni.'

'Excellent. I'll give you a referral to an endocrinologist in Melbourne.' He put on his mock-father voice. 'You do need to keep in touch with your doctor up there and have regular blood tests.'

Brittany gave him a high-wattage smile. 'Don't worry, mate, I'll be good, I never want to feel like that again.' She stood up, scoffed one last chip, waved and sauntered down the street.

Will laughed. It was so refreshing to be treated just as a doctor. The Laurelton Valley residents had been overwhelming in their welcome of him. He'd been invited to homes, judged the primary school's Parade of Fairytale Characters and had even helped out at the footy clinic. People seemed genuinely interested in him as a person rather than as someone whose name appeared annually on the 'Who's Rich?' list. He was enjoying being a regular bloke.

And the medicine challenged him, especially as a lot of it was adult medicine. It had been a couple of years since he'd practised that, and it took different skills.

Doctors in small towns knew about their patients' lives because they lived among them and he'd found himself doing quite a bit of counselling. Farmers had it tough and although Meg was brilliant at what she did, men seemed to prefer to talk to another man.

Some people might think writing repeat prescriptions was dull stuff but it involved an examination and a chat and he discovered all sorts of things that he'd been able to follow up on. Thankfully, emergencies like Brodie were few and far between. He made a mental note to call for another update on the baby's condition.

The other day he'd had a lot of fun at Meg's

healthy baby clinic when she'd been caught up trying to get a handle on the latest change-of-season lice outbreak at the school. He smiled at the memory of the indignant look on her face when he'd teased her, calling her the nit nurse.

Routine or not, he'd enjoyed it all. Medicine didn't have to be all drama and urgency. Medicine was people and he'd missed his patients, especially the kids.

A horn sounded, breaking into his thoughts, and he glanced up to see a smiling Meg winding down the ute's window. White heat flared, blood rushed to his groin. Her smile did dangerous things to him every single time and she seemed to have no idea.

She beckoned him over. 'Jump in.'

He picked up his medical bag and walked over to the ute. He leaned into the open window, breathing in the apple scent of her hair, using every ounce of restraint he had not to kiss her. 'Emergency?'

She laughed. 'No, this is a social call. The Patricks have some bantam hens for me and as we're quiet and it's Friday afternoon, I thought you could see a bit of the district and help me load the hens.'

'So, really, you're just using me for my manly strength?'

'Absolutely.'

Her wide-eyed gaze hooked with his, and the moment expanded. He recognised the longing in her eyes, and knew his need was reflected back to her. Somehow, and soon, he needed to get her out of town, somewhere private, where they could explore this simmering lust.

Meg dragged her eyes away from Will's, reluctantly breaking the moment but knowing it was totally necessary. Nothing could and nothing would happen between them.

She pushed open the passenger door. 'Get in. It's a short drive.'

The road followed the Laurelton River, which was flowing with icy water generated by melting snow. Round river stones, smoothed by the rush of water, reflected a series of browns and yellows through the clear water.

Meg glanced across at Will, whose sight seemed fixed on the view. 'Did you catch up with Sheryl Jettison and organise her blood-pressure medication?'

Will turned back from the window, the far-away look in his eye quickly replaced by alert attention. 'I'm trialling her on a new drug which hopefully will suit her better. It's had some great outcomes in clinical trials.'

Meg tilted her head. 'You've been doing some professional reading?'

A guarded look crossed his face. 'I keep up. Don't worry, I'm not likely to confuse liquorice all-sorts with blood-pressure medication.' Although it sounded like a joke, his tone didn't encourage further comment.

Meg respected the tone but only because they'd just arrived at the Patricks' gate. Now wasn't the time to pin Will down on exactly when he was planning to return to medicine. But she was determined to have that conversation because from what she'd observed over the last couple of weeks he was wasting his talents selling confectionery.

She swung the ute across the obligatory cattlegrid and pulled up in front of the house.

Surprise crossed Will's face. 'I didn't know farmhouses came so new and modern.'

She laughed. 'It's a lot different from Big Hill Farm, that's for sure. The Patricks have six sons, ranging from twenty-one down to four, and this house was Doug's gift to Sue on their twenty-fifth wedding anniversary. How she managed for so many years with an outhouse and a lean-to for a laundry I will never know.' She slammed the ute door closed. 'Come and meet Sue.'

Ten minutes later, surrounded by cups of tea, a huge platter of scones, farm cream and home-made raspberry jam, Meg sneaked a look at Will.

With true Laurel Valley hospitality, Sue was pressing him to accept a third helping of scones.

Will gave his trademark smile. 'Sue, I think you should enter these scones in the Royal Melbourne Show—the world needs to know about them.'

Sue blushed. 'Actually, Will, I have won a blue ribbon for my scones at the Laurelton Show.'

A darked-haired little boy appeared by his mother's side, clutching a truck and with a hopeful look in his eye. 'When are the kids coming home, Mum?'

'When the big hand is on the twelve and the little hand is on the four.' Sue pointed to the large kitchen clock.

'Oh, but that's *ages* away.' Dejected, his head dropped forward.

Sue turned to Will and Meg. 'The kinder year is a toughie. Josh is keen to be at big school and finds the afternoons rather long.'

Will moved off his chair and squatted down to the four-year-old's level, his back to the glass patio doors. 'That's a pretty good-looking truck you've got there.'

Josh nodded, his face serious. 'But the bull-dozer's got caterpillar wheels. You need that for the mud on our farm.'

'I bet you do. The truck would sink, wouldn't it?'

Meg's heart turned over in her chest. No wonder Will had chosen paediatrics—he was a natural with kids.

Josh squinted and rubbed his eyes and then looked at Will. 'Like when my dad tried to pull the tree stump out by the river.'

'There are no secrets with kids.' Sue laughed. 'Josh loves to tell everyone that story, much to Doug's embarrassment.'

Josh moved again so Will's body shaded him from the bright afternoon light streaming through the glass and busied himself with the trucks while Will lined up the crane and the front-end loader.

Will absently built a tower of blocks for the bulldozer. 'Sue, has Josh always avoided bright light?'

Sue thought for a moment. 'Actually, now you mention it, just lately he has moved his play area. He always used to play where you are now. Why do you ask?'

Meg looked at Will, trying to read his expression. He'd noticed something, she was sure of it, but what?

'Would you object to me examining his eyes?'

Sue started. 'No, of course not, I can bring him down to the clinic tomorrow. I was thinking of doing that anyway because one day last week I thought I saw a white spot on his eye, but it had gone the next time I looked so I thought I was imagining it.'

Will stood up. 'Actually, if it's all right with you, I'd like to do it now.'

Meg quietly slipped out of the door and pulled Will's medical kit out of the ute. When she returned she found Sue anxiously winding a teatowel through her hands and Will back playing with Josh.

Sue grabbed her hand. 'Will says he could see a reflection in Josh's pupil. That can't be good.'

Meg gave Sue's hand a reassuring squeeze. 'He's a good doctor, Sue. He wouldn't have mentioned this unless he thought it really important.'

Will wound the crane down so Josh could connect a load to the hook. 'I'm a doctor, Josh, and I'd like you to sit on Mum's knee for a minute so I can have a look at your eyes.'

The little boy silently considered the request.

Will backed a truck under the crane. 'You can look in my eyes first, if you like, with the special eye-looker.'

Josh's face lit up with a smile. 'Cool.' He stood up and then jumped up and down, waiting for his mother to sit. He quickly climbed onto his mother's lap and looked expectantly at Will.

In a few short minutes Will had gained the trust of this little boy and not a lolly in sight. Meg decided he was definitely wasting his talents in the business world.

She passed him the ophthalmoscope, heat rushing through her at his smile of thanks. Oh, she had to get a grip. She was worse than a fourteen-year-old with a crush.

'OK, mate, you look through the little hole into my eye.'

The instrument seemed large in Josh's pudgy hands but he very seriously peered through it as Will leaned close to him.

'Good job.' Will reached for the ophthalmoscope. 'Now it's my turn. Can you sit very still?'

The little boy seemed to sit a bit straighter on his mother's lap, taking on the responsibility of his part of the task.

Meg wished she could see Will's expression but his face was too close to Josh's, his right eye pressed against the 'scope.

'Now the other eye, mate, and we're done. You're doing a great job.'

Will seemed to take longer to examine the left

eye. 'Sorry, Josh, but I need to look at your other eye one more time. But you're being such a good guy that I'm sure Meg might be able to rustle up a lollypop out of my black bag.'

It was Meg's turn to smile. 'I sure can. I know just which pocket Dr Will keeps them in.'

'Have you got a red one?' Josh looked hopeful.

'There are lots of red ones.' This time her smile felt tight. If Will was rechecking the eye, he must have found something he wanted to compare.

A myriad of children's eye conditions ran through her mind. But Josh had no inflammation, no sign of injury, and his mother didn't seem to think he was having trouble seeing, so that ruled out retinal detachment. *I thought I saw a white spot on his eye.*

A horrendous thought embedded itself into her mind.

Will leant back and put the ophthalmoscope down. 'You can hop down now, buddy, and get your lollipop.' He tilted his head very slightly toward her, the movement almost imperceptible.

At that moment Meg knew Will had just given her the worst news possible. She held out her hand to Josh. 'Let's go over here and look in the bag.' While she let the little boy make his choice, her concentration focused completely on Will and Sue. She hadn't seen his face this serious since they'd been stuck on Mt Hume.

'Sue, your maternal instincts were correct. Josh does have a white spot on his eye and the "cat's-eye" type of reflection I saw fits in with that.'

Sue swallowed hard, her eyes firmly fixed on Will's face. 'It's not good news, is it?'

Will shook his head. 'No, I'm afraid it isn't. Josh will need more tests but I think he has a condition called retinoblastoma.' He took in a deep breath. 'Cancer of the eye.'

The mother's hands flew to her mouth. Disbelief and horror marred her already worried face. 'His beautiful eyes.' Her hand reached out toward Meg.

She immediately moved to Sue's side and gripped her hand. 'Sue, I'm so sorry.' The words sounded inadequate. She looked at Will. 'What now?'

'Josh has to go to Melbourne.'

Sue gasped. 'Can't he go to Winston? Melbourne is so far…'

Will's expression didn't change but Meg saw his sorrow for the situation in his eyes. 'Josh needs access to the top medical treatment in this area, and that's in Melbourne. He needs to have a full eye examination under general anaesthetic. He'll also need an ultrasound and a CT scan, as well as a lumbar puncture, to determine if the cancer is confined to the eye.'

'Oh, God, Melbourne… The boys…Doug…' Sue's face blanched white.

Meg's brain clicked into gear. 'Sue, you know the town will look after the children. I'll start a phone tree and I'm sure Emily Patterson will get a roster going.'

'Thanks.' She looked up at Will, tears misting her eyes. 'Will he lose his eye?' Susan whispered the words.

'I don't know. It depends on the size of the tumour or tumours. The first road of treatment is usually a combination of chemo and radiotherapy.' Will leaned forward. 'I can introduce you to the doctors who will be treating Josh. I know them all—I used to work with them.'

Meg should have been surprised at his gesture

of going to Melbourne with the Patricks, but she wasn't. The man truly cared for people. A tiny curl of envy unfolded deep inside her. He'd be gone for the weekend. She should feel relieved, but she didn't.

'That's very kind of you, Doctor.' She gripped Meg's hand even harder. 'But are you sure? I mean…'

'Meg and I wouldn't want you to be alone in Melbourne. You need a bit of Laurelton with you and we're both happy to come.' He spoke with the firmness of a man in charge.

Astonishment filled Meg. She couldn't go to Melbourne.

She opened her mouth to speak but his look silenced her. How could eyes the smooth, rich colour of melted chocolate with peppermint flecks look so determined and unyielding?

Will continued. 'Ring your husband and tell him about Josh. Meg and I will be back in half an hour and we'll leave as soon as possible.'

The stoic farmer's wife picked up her phone and started to dial.

Will stood up, glancing briefly over at Josh

who was happily sucking his lollypop and playing with his trucks. He put his hand under Meg's arm and propelled her out of the house and toward the ute.

He shoved his hands deep into his pockets in a distracted way. 'Just when I thought Laurelton was a quiet medical backwater, I get two kids who could lose their sight.'

Meg experienced his pain and frustration at the unfairness of life. 'You can visit Brodie when you're in Melbourne.'

His attention snapped back. 'Can you be ready to come to Melbourne for the weekend in about an hour?' His voice seemed deeper than usual.

She raised her brows. 'It's my reliever's weekend off and as you're planning to be in Melbourne for the weekend, I really can't leave Laurelton.'

'I can arrange for a doctor to be in town on the weekend.'

'Really?' She hated the tinge of sarcasm that came into her voice but the man had no idea. 'You think you can achieve what I and the bush nursing centre's community committee have tried to do for three years?' She clicked her fingers. 'Just like that?'

He nodded and punched some numbers into his mobile. 'I've got a few mates on the mountain who owe me a favour.' He grinned.

Before she could utter a word he turned slightly, put his phone to his ear and took a couple of steps. 'Andrew, mate, it's Will Cameron. Fancy a bit of locum work for a couple of days?'

Stunned, Meg leaned against the ute, trying to take it all in. She'd just witnessed Will Cameron, doctor, member of the A-list and philanthropist in action. She'd been completely organised by a man on a mission. Sue needed support and Will had made it happen.

She was more than happy to go with Sue and Josh. But a weekend in Melbourne, without her mother and all of Laurelton playing chaperone—how would she keep her distance?

She was about to find out.

Meg stared out toward the large park across the road from the hospital. At least she could see some trees in the concrete jungle that was Melbourne. She stifled a yawn. It had been a huge twenty-four hours.

Last night, after Josh had been admitted, she'd stayed with him and his mum, accompanying them to all Josh's tests and finally settling a very scared and overwhelmed little boy into the ward. Sue had insisted on sleeping on a fold-away bed next to Josh and Meg had finally fallen, fully clothed, into an exhausted sleep in the residents' quarters around three a.m.

But vivid dreams of Will riding a horse through the hospital corridors had kept waking her up.

That morning she'd breakfasted with Sue, keeping her company until Doug arrived. Right now the terrified couple were with Will, speaking with the oncologist.

Meg had stayed with Josh, entertaining him with some stories, but he'd fallen asleep. She yawned, wishing she could snuggle next to him and catch a snooze.

She longed for a bath and a sleep in a comfortable bed. If she could just stretch out and close her eyes…

Sue tapped Meg on the shoulder. 'Thanks for staying with him.'

Meg started. 'You're welcome. It was my pleasure.' It was such a small thing compared to what the Patricks faced.

'Will's organised and explained the medical treatments and the doctors and nurses are all wonderful.' Sue's voice caught. 'They say that Josh has a really strong chance of getting through this.'

Meg reached out and silently hugged her. Feeling some of Sue's grief, thinking about her own. Wishing she had a child to hold and cherish. Knowing she could only sense a tiny part of Sue's pain.

The mother straightened her shoulders. 'I really appreciate you staying, but I don't want to hold you up any more. Doug's sister is due any minute and my cousins from Footscray are coming in this afternoon, so we won't be alone. Off you go and enjoy your weekend.'

Meg searched the woman's face. 'Are you sure?'

Susan nodded. 'Of course. You've done more than enough.' She suddenly looked over Meg's shoulder. 'And so have you, Will—you've both done more than enough. You might be from the city but you've got country values.'

'It was our pleasure.' Will's rich voice vibrated behind Meg as he came to stand very close to her.

She looked up at him. Delight at Sue's praise played across his face dancing across the black stubble, darker around his mouth, making him more handsome than ever. Her breath caught in her throat and she coughed.

Will gave her a gentle pat on the back, his touch making her dizzy.

Sue crossed her arms. 'Look after her, Will. She works too hard.'

Will grinned. 'I intend to.' His face became more serious. 'Take care, Sue, and call me any time.'

'I will. Now, go.' Sue moved her hands back and forth, shooing them away.

Meg stepped forward as Sue wouldn't let her stay where she was. As she started walking toward the lifts, Will fell silently into step with her, his hands shoved deep into his pockets. She glanced at him. 'Thinking about Josh?'

He nodded. 'The treatment is pretty rugged

but we've caught it early. He's got a good chance of keeping his eye.'

Hope and relief collided inside her. 'He's lucky you spotted it.' She pushed the button to summon the lift and stifled a yawn.

He gave her a tired smile. 'The residents' quarters aren't the best place for a decent sleep, are they?'

She stepped into the empty lift. 'No. I'd kill for a soft bed and a feather pillow.'

Will followed her and the doors closed behind them. He stepped in close. 'You won't have to kill. I've got the perfect bed waiting for you.'

Her heart hammered erratically at his husky voice. His eyes radiated desire and longing, his stare sending tendrils of sweet sensation through her. Every skerrick of fatigue vanished instantly.

The ping of the lift heralding the opening doors surprised her into action. She walked out of the lift and across the foyer in a daze, blinking at the bright spring sunshine as she stepped outside.

Will's hand slipped under her elbow and guided her into a taxi. It was almost as if she was out of her body, looking in. It all seemed unreal.

'The Langtree Hotel, please.' Will directed the taxi driver to the boutique hotel.

She should speak. *Say something.* They were going to one of Melbourne's most expensive hotels. She couldn't afford it. She didn't want Will paying for her, but she refused to have an argument in the taxi, in front of a bemused driver. So she stayed silent and stared out the window at the skyscrapers that defined the cosmopolitan city.

Three minutes later a doorman opened her car door. The braid on his jacket sparkled as he moved aside, allowing her to exit. She stepped out onto the pavement.

'Afternoon, Dr Cameron.' The doorman tipped his hat.

Will knew the doorman? That stunned her. How often did he stay here? *Who did he stay here with?* The traitorous thought crept in. *You shouldn't even care who he might have been here with,* Miss Sensible countered.

Meg gave herself a shake—this was getting all too weird.

'Hello, Gregory. How's the new baby?' Will

walked around to Meg and curved his arm proprietorially around her waist. With gentle pressure he edged her forward.

Swirls of heat travelled through her.

Gregory opened the front door of the hotel. 'Gorgeous, sir. Takes after me.' He laughed. 'I've got photos at the concierge desk when you've got some time.'

'Excellent. I'll catch them later.'

And he would. Meg knew enough of Will to know how much genuine interest he took in other people. She walked into a foyer that was dominated by the fragrance of fresh flowers. Bunches of cream freesias clustered in rectangular glass vases giving off a pungent perfume. Purple, pink and white tulips rested in blue and white vases, which resided on polished red gum tables.

But before she could take it all in or catch her breath, Will, with a quick wave to the staff at the reception desk, headed her toward a broad, carpeted staircase.

She needed to speak. *Now* was the time to speak. Mr Organisation needed to be pulled up short. His assumption that they would share a room irked part of her. She would have liked to have been asked!

He dropped his arm from her waist and pulled an old-fashioned key out of his pocket. 'This is what I love about this place—real keys, not those plastic cards.'

'Will, I really don't think that this—'

The door swung open. Her bag rested on the luggage stand. The floral cover on the queen-sized bed was turned down. *I've got the perfect bed waiting for you.*

'This is your room. I hope you like it. I'm across the hall.'

Her indignation came to a sudden halt. Disappointment rammed into it. Separate rooms. For ten minutes she'd been certain he was planning on them sharing a room. Her head spun as surprise sent blood rushing to her feet.

'You've got this one because it's got a spa, and after the night you've had I thought you'd love a long soak.' He grinned.

She struggled to organise her thoughts and speak in a coherent way. 'Will, I can't afford to stay here and—'

'Hey, I insisted you come down to help Sue and Josh. Consider the room a thank-you.'

'I really think that...' Her voice trailed off as he closed the small gap between them. Every nerve ending went into overload and her brain stalled. All she could think of was Will. His masculine scent enveloped her, his eyes zeroed in on hers, dark with lust, and his hand brushed her own. An ache of longing deepened inside her, creating an emptiness she wanted desperately to be filled.

His head dipped low and she moved her own to receive his kiss. Yearning for his touch and taste.

But his lips spoke whispered words instead. 'Consider it a repayment of Big Hill Farm hospitality.' He stepped back briskly and moved across the hall, opening his door.

Regret surged inside her, mixing with frustration and disappointment. For three long weeks she'd tried to resist the amazingly strong attraction that consumed her. She tried to rationalise it—it only existed because of the trauma they had shared. After his last kiss she'd let him walk away from her, telling herself that pursuing him would only end in tears.

But a moment ago she'd seen he wanted her. That knowledge gave her power.

She didn't want to be in her room and know he was across the hall in his. For seven nights she'd lain in her bed, in her mother's house, picturing Will asleep across the hall, her mother's presence acting as a natural brake on her actions.

But, hell, she was an adult. There were no stars in her eyes anymore—Graeme had doused those. Will had told her he had no plans to marry, no plans for a long-term relationship. Even if he'd changed his mind, he wouldn't choose her. She couldn't give him a child and he'd want a family. He loved kids.

But this wasn't happy families, she knew that. This was reality. This was unmistakable lust.

She had needs, just like the next woman. She'd just survived a plane crash. Life was fickle and unreliable. She wanted him and now she was certain he wanted her. While they were in Laurelton nothing could happen because the town was too small. But this was Melbourne. And, damn it, this time she was taking what she wanted, even if it was only for a day and a night.

'Will.'

He turned at the almost strangled sound of his name, his gaze catching hers. He wanted to sink into her gorgeous eyes, which seemed larger and more luminous than ever. Her smooth cheeks glowed pink and her plump lips demanded to be kissed.

It had been a Herculean effort not to kiss her a moment ago. But this time he wasn't rushing her. Unlike their picnic in the snow, this time he was going slowly. She deserved to be loved long and languorously and in complete comfort.

She walked toward him, her eyes simmering with desire, her expression oddly determined. She reached her hand up and touched his stubble-rough cheek. 'The plane crash proved to me that life is short. I don't want to be sensible. I don't want a room of my own. I want you.' She stood on tiptoe and pulled his head down to hers, her lips melding to his in a rush of heat.

Blood raced to his groin, the kiss igniting his barely contained passion. 'I can't offer you anything more than these few weeks.'

'I know. Let's call it "post-plane crash therapy".'

Joy raced through him and he kissed her hard, pulling her to him. Reluctantly he pulled away, but the need to touch her, stay connected to her, burned strong. With one hand holding hers, he somehow managed to unlock his door with his other hand. He pulled her into the room, wrapping his arms around her.

She hesitated, anxiety skating over her face, and she bit her lip. 'Will, about condoms…'

He stroked her cheek, understanding her concern. 'It's all sorted. I wouldn't hurt you for the world.'

'Thank you.' Her eyes sparkled the bright blue of a pacific sea. Placing her hands behind his neck, she ran trails of kisses along his cheek, her lips working their magic, stunning him, making his knees weak.

They fell onto the bed.

'You've reduced me to this, a man who can barely stand.'

She grinned wickedly and reached for the buttons on his shirt. 'I've wanted to explore this chest since I saw you in my kitchen wearing a T-shirt and holding a pile of wood.'

'Be my guest.' The words came out on a croak.

She undid the top button, folded his shirt back and kissed the exposed skin. As she lifted her lips her tongue darted out, licking the area lightly. She undid the second button and repeated the action.

Stars exploded in his head.

She pushed him gently back onto the bed and straddled him. 'It's a big job, but someone's got to do it.' Her slim fingers disengaged button three, and button four. Where her fingers touched, her lips followed.

He gave himself up to the sensory overload, soaking up her touch, savouring the fresh fruity smell of her hair as it caressed his skin, watching the expressions of wonder cross her face as she undid each button. He'd imagined this moment for so long, but reality far exceeded expectation.

Her tongue wrought havoc, making the touch of her fingers feel chaste. The final button popped and her hands raced all over his skin.

Heat on heat.

Sensation building on sensation, tingling through every part of him.

For a brief moment her fingers paused. She

gazed down at him, her eyes wide and clear. Desire, need and power interplayed. He knew she wanted him as much as he wanted her.

He moved like a panther stalking prey, rolling her over in one quick movement, laughing at the indignation on her beautiful face.

'Hey, I hadn't finished.' She pursed her lips in mock annoyance. 'There was a belt that followed on from the buttons.'

'If those fingers were planning an assault down there, then this might all be over mighty quick.'

'Is that right? Where's your self-control?' Her rich, teasing laugh surrounded him.

His left hand, which rested against her back, flicked open her bra hooks. His right hand swooped under her T-shirt and cupped her breast, his thumb gently grazing her nipple, which quickly hardened.

A shocked gasp left her lips.

He raised his brows in mock surprise. 'Where's your self-control?'

'You're not playing fair.'

He grinned. 'Sweetie, I play to please.' He pulled the T-shirt over her head and pulled the bra away, dropping it onto the floor.

Bending his head, he captured her breast in his mouth, his tongue caressing and sucking. He felt her shudder beneath him. The knowledge he could make her react like this expanded inside him, filling the spaces of loneliness he hadn't known he had.

Her hands played all over his back, her touch alternating between feather-like caresses and frantic clutching, depending on what his mouth was doing to her breast.

Her voice, heavy with need, broke the heat-filled silence. 'Too many clothes.'

He popped the top button on her jeans and pulled them down. His hands outlining the sweet curve of her bottom which he'd come to explore. He dumped the jeans next to the bra.

His stunned gaze zeroed in on a tiny triangle of cream lace.

Meg giggled. 'Your look is priceless. You expected practical cotton undies, didn't you?' A sexy smile played around her lips. 'Country girls are full of surprises.'

'I'm learning that.' His fingers stroked the edge of the lace, slowly making their way underneath to the treasure it hid.

He stroked her, his fingers wet with her need.

She bucked toward him, all traces of the teasing look gone. She threw her head back, her eyes wide with wanting, and a moan of pleasure rent the air.

He couldn't believe it was possible to harden any more than he had, but he did. Excitement that he could do this to her, bring her this much pleasure, kept him in control. Barely.

He wanted to enter her, wanted to feel her around him, but this was her moment. He kept stroking, his gaze fixed on her, watching her experience what she so deserved.

She shuddered against him as waves of sensation built and built to fever pitch. She wanted to feel him inside her, wanted to grip him tightly. 'Will.'

'Shush, this one's for you.' His gaze never left hers.

His fingers never let up their delicious stroking, his kisses trailed sweetness against her breasts, and she gave in to the pleasure. The sweet explosions rolled through her in waves and her lips cried out his name.

She opened her eyes to see his grinning face.

'You're good.'

'I know.'

She laughed. He'd just given her the best orgasm she'd ever known, and he knew it. 'I need to return the favour.' Her hands reached for his pants.

He groaned. 'I'll take them off.' He removed them quickly, and knelt before her, hard and splendid.

She ached to feel him, all of him. She reached out her hand.

He groaned again. 'I'm running out of self-control here.'

Guilt pierced her. He'd been so selfless for her. She kissed him hard, feeling him against her belly, and pushed at his arms.

He fell back onto the bed and she moved across him, applying the condom, and then felt him enter her, filling her with himself, and with his essence. She took him and held him, and moved against him again and again, building the pressure.

Lights danced in her head, the vortex of pleasure whirling her and Will together higher and higher until they exploded together in a moment of extreme bliss.

As the cascades of sensation poured through her she savoured the moment, wishing it could last for ever.

CHAPTER NINE

THE machines of Intensive Care beeped and pinged and Meg rested her head on the outside of Brodie's humidicrib. Will had suggested they pop in and visit him before they headed back to Laurelton.

For someone who was a locum, he really seemed to have an amazing capacity to care for her town. What if he really loved Laurelton? What if he decided to stay?

Get real. He belongs in Melbourne, he has a life there. She breathed out, blowing away the crazy and unrealistic thought, focusing on Brodie. 'At least he's no longer being nursed on the open cot.'

Will's penetrating gaze met hers. 'It's a good sign. It's been a rough couple of weeks for Sally.'

'In more ways than one.' She felt the reassuring pressure of Will's arm tighten around her as a glimmer of her old pain of infertility threatened to rise. It stalled at his thoughtfulness.

'Remember you're a totally gorgeous woman.' The words spoken softly were intended to soothe.

Memories of their lovemaking swamped her. He'd been the most amazing lover—kind, considerate, inventive. She smiled at what he could do with his mouth.

The weekend had whizzed past in a blur of love-making, with long conversations while cuddled up in the spa, and in glorious, peaceful sleep in Will's comforting arms.

She couldn't believe how well she'd slept. Since the plane crash she'd had insomnia, but even before then there had been many nights when she'd tossed and turned more than she'd slept. She was very familiar with three a.m., lying awake worrying about the bank repayments, about a patient whose condition concerned her, about the unexpected direction of her life.

Will's presence filled her with a peace she'd never known. A peace that soothed and scared her.

Will stepped away and Meg looked up.

An exhausted-looking Sally walked toward

them, two paces in front of her husband, Mark, who looked completely shattered. 'Thanks for visiting us and staying with Brodie while we talked to the specialist.'

Will's hazel eyes scanned Sally's face. 'Do you understand everything he said?'

Sally nodded. 'Brodie's over the worst. We just have to wait and see—only time will tell about his eyesight.'

Meg reached out and hugged the woman. 'Let's hope Brodie's back in Laurelton in a couple of weeks.'

Mark spoke gruffly. 'Thanks for being in Laurelton, Dr Cameron.'

Will shook his hand. 'I was glad to help.'

'Will you still be there when Brodie comes home?' Sally spoke hopefully.

Meg glanced at Will, whose face had suddenly become impassive.

He seemed to hesitate. 'No, I'll be back in Melbourne then.'

Remember, you and Will being together is fantasy. Meg dragged in a deep breath. She knew her time with him was temporary. It had to be, but she planned to hold off the real world for as long as possible and savour every single minute.

'Are you just about ready to go?' Will stood in the doorway of Meg's office.

'Hometime already?'

She put down her pen, glanced up at him and stretched, her shirt pulling tightly across her chest, outlining the round curves of her breasts, which he knew intimately.

Blood shot to his groin. She was so totally delectable. It was hard work keeping his hands off her. But he had little choice during working hours when the clinic was full of patients.

However, they'd all gone home now and he'd locked the front door. And the back. 'Yep, it's almost six and you've been here since eight.' He walked around behind her and rested his hands on her shoulders, massaging the tension away.

She put her hand on top of his and tilted her head back, looking up at him, her smile enticing.

He dropped a kiss onto her forehead.

She swivelled on her chair and captured his head with her hands, pressing her soft lips against his. Her tongue nibbled at his bottom lip, seeking entry to his mouth.

He groaned. He needed to touch her, feel her. He pulled her out of the chair and into his arms, holding her tightly against him, loving the way her body curved against his.

He opened his mouth, blending his heat with hers, marvelling at how her enthusiasm and passion for life crossed over into their lovemaking.

The pressure of her kiss lessened and she pulled back, her breathing fast and hard, her pupils large black discs.

Disappointment slugged him at the brevity of the kiss.

She gave him a wry smile. 'You've forgotten, haven't you?'

As her finger trailed down his jaw, cascades of tingling sensations exploded inside him, making him forget everything.

She continued. 'I'm working tonight, moderating the "Give up Smoking" group. They'll be arriving pretty soon.'

Frustration threaded through him. He'd been planning a secret seduction. Since coming back from Melbourne they hadn't had a lot of alone time. He'd had to be content with a stolen kiss here and there. Not that he didn't enjoy those— he just wanted a lot more.

And he only had a week left in Laurelton.

Staying at Big Hill Farm dampened any plans of a replication of the passion they'd shared in Melbourne. As much as he liked Eleanor, having Meg's mother in the house wasn't conducive to lovemaking. Still, he looked forward to each evening after Eleanor had gone to bed and he and Meg cuddled on the couch and talked. He'd never met anyone he could talk to quite the way he could talk to Meg. Her quick wit and sense of humour meant rapid repartee, and yet he could still have deep and serious discussions with her about all sorts of things.

Except about Camerons and Dad.

'Will?'

Concentrating on Meg's voice drove the nagging thought out of his head. 'Sorry.' He breathed out. 'So, you're working.'

She smiled at his wistful tone. 'We both know Melbourne was make-believe. I'll be home

around eight. Mum's expecting you for dinner.'
Her lips grazed his in a fleeting kiss as a
pounding sounded on the clinic door. 'Open that
on your way out, please.'

He'd been organised and despatched. And he
couldn't do a damn thing about it.

Jet bounded out to meet him as he parked the car.
He loved dogs, but inner-city living wasn't dog
friendly. He enjoyed the convenience of his
serviced apartment at the Langtree but maybe he
should look for something else. Something with
a courtyard.

Why? Are you thinking Meg might like that?

The thought rocked him. He and Meg were
just a temporary thing, part of getting through
the trauma of surviving a near-death experience. *We both know Melbourne was make-
believe.* Both of them had said they were not
in the market for a relationship. His life was in
Melbourne. She belonged in the bush,
gorgeous and free.

Except she wasn't free. She wore the pain of
her childlessness in her eyes every day. He saw

it. He wished he could change that. Give her back her dreams.

But he couldn't, and both of them needed to get back onto the paths of their lives, the ones they had been treading before the crash. His time in Laurelton was almost over.

He pulled open the wire door, walked into the back porch and put his bag down on the boot box. 'Hi, Eleanor,' he called out loudly, to let her know he was home.

He filled Jet's bowl with food, ruffled the fur on her head and stepped into the kitchen. Usually, Eleanor was cooking dinner or sitting reading at the table. The kitchen lacked the signs of food preparation. He looked out the window. The chooks were still roaming free, which was unusual at this time of night. A prickle of unease made him shiver. Perhaps she was resting.

'Eleanor.' He walked down the hall, his footsteps sounding loud on the Baltic pine boards. 'Are you here?' He checked the lounge room. The TV was on but there was no sign of Eleanor.

He went back to the table and checked for a note. Nothing. He marched back down the hall and knocked on her bedroom door. No reply. He opened the door. 'Eleanor?' He walked in but the room was empty.

Unease turned into full-blown concern. He started opening guest rooms, working through the five rooms systematically, including his own. All were made up in anticipation of occupancy but Eleanor wasn't in any of them.

Meg's room.

He hammered on the door. 'Eleanor?' He pushed it open.

He walked around the bed. She lay on the floor, her crutches beside her and her right leg splayed out at a strange angle.

He dropped to his knees, worried about her conscious state. 'Hell, Eleanor.' He jiggled her shoulder.

Her eyes fluttered open, dark in her pale face. Her dry lips looked about to crack. 'Will, thank goodness. I knew Meg was working late…'

'What happened?' His hand reached for her wrist to check her pulse.

'I fell this morning. I came in here, looking for a book, and I used the stepladder to get it off the top shelf. I lost my balance and I think my leg is broken.' Her eyes fluttered closed, exhaustion and pain etched on her face.

Sympathy and concern sat heavy in his stomach. 'I'll be right back. I'll just grab my bag.'

As he ran down the corridor he used his mobile phone and rang for an ambulance. He'd do a full examination in a minute but it didn't take a medical degree to see either the leg or hip was broken.

He grabbed his bag and headed back to the room. 'I'm going to put an IV in first, Eleanor, because I'm worried about dehydration. Do you have any cardiac problems?' He wrapped a tourniquet around her upper arm.

'I'm on blood-pressure medication.'

He nodded, acknowledging her answer, and swabbed her forearm. 'This will hurt a bit as I slide the needle in.'

She bit her lip and breathed out deeply.

The cannula slid in, and he quickly connected a normal saline drip, hanging the bag on Meg's coatstand.

He picked up her wrist to check her pulse again. 'What's the pain like?'

'Actually, it's not sharp, more like a dull ache in my groin.'

'I can give you something for it.' He laid her hand gently on her stomach, and then pulled a pillow off the bed to put under her head.

'I'll see how I go.' She spoke the words firmly.

'You don't have to be stoic, Eleanor. It might hurt while I examine you and it will definitely hurt when I strap your legs together.'

'If it gets too much, I'll let you know—deal?'

He heard the same intonation in her voice as Meg's. The suck-it-down-and-deal-with-it approach to life. 'Deal.'

He examined the leg and her hip. 'Does it hurt here?' He pressed on the upper thigh.

She flinched. 'Yes.'

'Well, an X-ray is the only conclusive way to diagnose but I think you've fractured your neck of femur—your hip. So it's hospital, surgery and rehab, I'm afraid.'

She let out a long, shuddering sigh. 'Well, I might get a bit of rest, I suppose.' She gave him a tired smile.

He studied the deep lines on her face that life

had placed there. She'd coped with the death of her husband and a chronic illness. 'Are you feeling weary, Eleanor?'

Her gaze hovered on his face for a moment and indecision swam in her eyes. She took in a breath. 'I am. Just lately, running the B&B has got hard. I've kept going for John's memory and for Meg. She loves the farm and so do I, but…'

He'd often wondered how she coped with her MS and working so hard. 'But you fancy something less hard going?'

She nodded. 'I've loved the life I've had here but each month it gets harder to meet the mortgage. With the snow season almost over, things are too tight. As it is, Meg's working seven days a week.'

He rested back on his heels. 'It doesn't seem to bother her, working the hours she does.'

Eleanor fixed him with a look only a mother could give. 'But it's not the life she should have. I know she always thought she'd raise a family in this house, like her father and I did, but that isn't going to happen and we have to accept it.' She sighed. 'I've been thinking about selling the farm and moving into town. It gets lonely out here and I've got friends in town.'

Will checked the flow of the IV, disquiet edging in. 'Does Meg know how you feel?'

An anxious expression crossed her face. 'No.'

He spoke carefully. 'Don't you think you should tell her?'

Her face crumpled. 'She's had enough heartache in the last couple of years.'

Will gave her a direct gaze. 'She loves you. She'll understand.'

Eleanor put her hand on his sleeve. 'This farm is so much a part of her. She's lost one dream already. I don't want to have to tell her she's lost another one.'

The love in her eyes for her daughter shone brightly yet he knew deep down that protecting Meg like this was not the solution to this problem.

He sighed at the complicated situations families got themselves into. 'I'm going to splint your leg now.' He started to wrap her legs together from the knees to the upper thigh, rolling the crêpe bandages carefully around her legs, trying not to move them too much.

She stiffened and flinched.

He paused. 'Are you doing OK?'

'If you've nearly finished, I am.'

He taped the end of the bandage in place. 'The road to Winston is pretty bumpy, and you don't need those corrugations vibrating through the fracture. I'll give you some pethidine and you can hopefully sleep all the way there.'

'Will.' Eleanor's voice held a plea. 'Promise me you won't tell Meg that I'm thinking about selling the farm.'

He squeezed her hand. 'I promise. I'll leave that to you. I'll only tell her you broke your hip.'

He only hoped she would tell Meg sooner than later.

Meg rubbed her aching eyes and tried to focus on the bills that needed to be paid. It had been a long, long Saturday. All her plans for a final weekend with Will had faded after Eleanor's accident. She'd spent the day visiting her mother in Winston hospital. The surgery had gone well and physiotherapy had started, but Eleanor would have to stay in Winston for quite a few weeks.

Jet sat by her side, her chin resting on top of Meg's feet in a cosy, comforting way. The house seemed eerily quiet. Without her mother there during the day, she'd had to cancel the last few bookings of the season so the usual chatter of guests had been silenced.

She glanced at the clock. Will had said he'd be home by seven. He'd been elusive about where he was going but he was a free agent, it was his day off, so he could go wherever he liked. She didn't have to know. *Yeah, right, you desperately want to know.*

But she had no right to ask. They weren't really together, they just shared an amazing short-term attraction.

His time in Laurelton was almost over. He'd promised three weeks and he'd delivered. She expected his departure any day. He hadn't mentioned it and she hadn't brought the subject up. It was almost as if they believed if it wasn't spoken of it wouldn't happen.

But it would happen and she wasn't looking forward to it.

The last few days—apart from the worry about

her mother—had been wonderful. They'd had the farmhouse to themselves, made love in almost every room, cooked meals together and shared the home paddock tasks. And they'd argued over the sections of the paper, just like other couples.

They'd been a couple.

The thought exploded inside her, stunning her. But they weren't a couple. He was leaving. She was staying.

Focus on the things you can control. Meg opened the cheque-book and systematically paid the bills, finding a sense of security in the orderliness of the paperwork. After banging the last stamp on an envelope she pulled over the bank statement and started to reconcile her mother's cheque-book.

She looked at her first attempt of adding up the row of figures. She blinked a couple of times. She must be more tired than she'd thought. She pressed the calculator's 'on' button and re-entered the figures.

The same number she'd calculated mentally came up on the screen.

A feeling of dread crawled over her skin. She pulled over the manila folder with previous bank statements. Riffling though each one, she saw that each month the overdraft had been extended further and further.

Her mother had never said a thing. Had never asked her for more money. Meg had assumed the B&B was at least covering costs. She found an envelope with the bank's letterhead attached to the back of a statement. With trembling hands she withdrew the sheet of paper.

It was a letter of default. Unless a significant amount was paid off the farm's mortgage, the farm would have to be sold.

Bile rose in her throat. Her farm. First she'd lost the dream to fill the house with children. Now it looked like she would lose the farm completely.

The front doorbell rang. Startled, Meg quickly shoved the paperwork into the manila folder. She wasn't expecting anyone and Will always used the back door.

She walked down the long hall. For a brief moment she thought she could smell jasmine rice but discounted that as a ridiculous thought. She pulled open the door.

Will's smiling face greeted her, his laughter at her confusion enveloping her as he pulled her into his arms. 'Do you fancy Thai food?'

'Sure, but not the three-hour drive to get it.' She let herself be wrapped in his arms, soaking up his touch, letting it ward off reality and the pain of what she'd just discovered.

'I ordered in.'

He spun her around and walked her toward the lounge room. Opening the door, he ushered her through. An open fire glowed in the grate, giving off waves of heat. Scented candles, their wicks burning brightly, sat at intervals along the mantel-piece, their aroma of sandalwood filling the room.

Two large cushions waited next to the coffee-table, which was covered in steaming bowls of fragrant Thai food. The pungent smell of fresh coriander assaulted her nostrils. Two glasses of champagne stood invitingly, the tiny bubbles whizzing up the length of the flutes.

Wonder and surprise rolled through her. 'I thought I could smell jasmine rice.' She laughed. 'How did you organise the food and set the room up?'

He smiled a secret smile. 'I've got contacts.'

'I bet you have.' She said the words lightly but she knew he would have contacts. She'd seen him in action both in Laurelton and Melbourne. Will Cameron commanded a certain amount of power when he wanted to use it.

'Sit.' He gestured to the cushions.

She sat as commanded.

He sat down next to her and handed her a glass of champagne. He tilted his glass and clinked it against hers. 'To surviving.'

She knew what he meant but sadness settled over her as she matched his words. She drank, letting the bubbles fizz on her tongue. She could think of many other things to toast, such as 'To three wonderful weeks', or 'To friendship', but she understood why he'd said survival. He'd never made her a promise of anything more than these few weeks.

Before she could dwell too long on the words, Will started to fill her bowl with a myriad of amazing foods.

He handed her a fork and a spoon. 'Aren't you glad it's Thai and you don't have to cope with chopsticks?'

She laughed. 'I always end up with more food in my lap than in my mouth and I wouldn't want to waste any of this. It smells delicious.'

For a few minutes they focused on the food, eating in companionable silence. There wasn't a Thai restaurant within a three-hour drive from Laurelton so she had no idea how he'd produced the meal but she was pretty certain all the effort in surprising her meant he was leaving. 'So, you're off to Melbourne?' She tried not to sound the way she really felt—needy and sad—but upbeat and conversational.

He put his empty plate down on the table and picked up her hand. 'Tomorrow morning.'

A tiny tear ripped in her heart. 'Well, I guess your dad needs you back at the helm.'

He nodded. 'My crash-recovery leave is over. I belong back in Melbourne.' His expression was almost neutral, betrayed only by the air of tension that she remembered being part of him when he'd first arrived in Laurelton.

She raised her brows. 'In a job where there isn't a patient in sight?'

'In a job where I can meet my family responsibilities and fund medical research so kids like Josh can be saved.' His clipped tone was back. The tone he developed whenever their discussion moved around to his job.

She leaned forward. 'Will, you're sensational with kids, you should be working at the coalface. Surely what you're doing now can be done by someone else?'

'It's not that simple.'

'It's not that hard. You hand over the reins and you go back to your specialisation and qualify.'

He suddenly brought her hand to his mouth, kissing the palm, his lips and tongue working their magic.

Liquid heat poured through her and her knees wobbled, even though she wasn't standing. Somehow, through this fog of desire she recognised his behaviour. Whenever they'd talked about his job and she'd pressed him about it, he'd changed the subject or pelted her with snowballs. She wouldn't let him get away with it this time.

'Will?'

His lips were now raining kisses along her forearm. He didn't stop, just mumbled, 'Hmm?'

'Explain to me "family responsibilities".'

He stiffened and met her gaze, the desire in his eyes clearing. 'You're not going to let me seduce you before I tell you, are you?' He dropped her hand.

'Probably not, no.'

A quick frown creased his brow, and then cleared. He spoke lightly. 'That's pretty strong bargaining power, although what if I chose not to seduce you and kept the information to myself?'

She put her hand on his knee and trailed her fingers slowly upward along his inner thigh. 'You could do that.'

His hand swooped, covering hers, stopping it on its trail upward to his groin. 'You strike a hard bargain.' With his other hand he picked up his champagne and downed the remains.

'Dad almost died from kidney failure. He'd been on the transplant list for a long time. I was a match to be a donor but both my parents refused to accept that gift. Instead, Dad asked me for my help in another way, my help to run the company until he was well again.' He sighed. 'I couldn't refuse him that. I'm glad I didn't. For the first time in my life I've really got to know my father. I genuinely like him. We get along pretty well.'

Family ties bound tightly, Meg knew that. She could see the attraction of taking the opportunity to get close to a man who had been a relatively absent father. Perhaps his father was enjoying a similar relationship with his son. 'When did your father get his transplant?'

'Four months ago, and he's doing pretty well now.'

From the moment she'd met Will he'd had an air of discontent about him and she was certain it was tied up with him leaving medicine, despite the fact he'd told her the job at Camerons was going well. She didn't hold back, she wanted to get to the bottom of this. 'So technically he's healthy enough to take over the running of Camerons again?'

He dropped her hand and his voice became defensive. 'Yes and no. He gets tired. I said I'd stay until he could do the job again.'

Meg remembered the frail-looking man who had collected Will after the crash. 'What if he's never well enough to take over?'

He stiffened. 'Sometimes your family needs you. Dad asked for help. You're making it sound all bad. It's not. I'm still involved in medicine through KKC.' He shrugged as if this wasn't a big deal. 'I'm helping in a different way. Sometimes our dreams have to deviate from our original plan.' •

He fixed her with a long stare. 'But I'm not telling you anything new about that, am I? Your dream was to have this farmhouse full of children, the way it was when you were a kid.'

His words struck home. She nodded, amazed he'd worked that out about her. 'This house used to be so alive with the high spirits of children.' She pushed her jaw out slightly. 'It still is in the school holidays.'

'But it isn't your original plan, is it?' He raised his brows as if to say, *So don't give me grief about my change.* His voice developed a caring softness. 'How viable is your plan to keep the farm going?'

Her mind darted back to the manila folder on the kitchen table. 'Just because some things take a lot of hard work and determination, it doesn't mean they're not worth doing. This farm has been in my family for a long time and I'm not going to be the Watson that loses it.' She clenched her fist. 'I think I'd do just about anything to keep the farm.'

A flash of something she couldn't totally read raced across his face. Was it sympathy? There was no reason for sympathy so she'd obviously misread it.

'But you said your brothers aren't interested in the farm, and now Eleanor's health is failing.'

A wave of concern started to break inside her but she stomped on it. She and her mother were a team. 'Mum broke her hip, which will heal. The physio said she'll be fine to come home. It's not like her MS has got worse. Besides, Mum wouldn't consider living anywhere else.'

He looked as if he was going to speak, but instead he ran his fingers down her cheek. 'This is our last night together, so why are we talking?' He pulled her into his lap and wrapped her legs around his waist. 'I was in the middle of seducing you before you rudely interrupted.'

His mouth joined hers in a kiss. A coaxing, sweet kiss, almost innocent in its intent, sending showers of joy cascading inside her, driving away her need to talk.

She let his mouth play against her own, savouring every part of the kiss, letting it flow over her, memorising it in all its wondrous detail. He ran his tongue along her bottom lip, caressing and teasing, making her body melt against his.

She opened her mouth to him, needing to experience his tongue dancing with hers, wanting his taste of champagne and desire to flood her. Willing the kiss to last for ever.

Knowing it couldn't.

But they had all night.

'Do you want to stay here?' His words murmured against her mouth.

The candles and the fire glowed, warming the room, making it a haven from the real world she had to face tomorrow. Tonight she could imagine she lived in her beloved home with the man of her dreams. 'Yes, here is good.' She lay back on the cushions and pulled him with her.

He tortured her with his tongue, driving her need for him to fever pitch. A moan of pleasure escaped her lips.

'You have no idea how much I've wanted to do this to you all day.' His husky voice washed over her.

'I've wanted it, too.' She kissed him hard, as if the pressure would change everything and stop him from leaving.

Farewell lovemaking should be slow. It should be languid and unrushed, something to treasure in the long evenings ahead that faced her.

But it wasn't.

They came together in a rush of tangled clothes, unsated need and a desperate ache for connectedness.

She gasped when he entered her, arching up to meet him, needing him inside her, gripping him and making him part of her.

Completing her.

Together they rose on a spiral of overwhelming pleasure until they shattered and floated back down to earth, holding each other tightly.

As they lay beside the fire, Will pulled a blanket over them and cuddled her close, likes spoons in a drawer. His strong arms encasing her just like they had in the snow cave a few short weeks before.

She loved being in his arms.

She loved him.

The thought sneaked in and exploded in her head. No! She couldn't love him. He was leaving. His life was in Melbourne, tangled up in his sense of duty and his family's business. She couldn't offer him anything. He didn't want a relationship.

They were each other's 'post-trauma' recovery programmes.

This was supposed to have been something to banish the unsettled feelings after the crash, to make her feel like a woman again.

But it was so much more.

She'd fallen in love despite her best intentions not to. But how could she have stayed aloof from this caring doctor, this wonderful man and amazing lover? He brightened her day. He was the last thing she thought about at night and the first thing she thought of when she woke, and he filled her dreams in between.

And tomorrow he would leave her house, but not her heart.

Surviving the crash suddenly seemed easy.

Will snuggled against Meg's body, marvelling at how the curve of her bottom fitted so snugly against him. He wasn't looking forward to tomorrow.

He knew he had to leave. The text messages notifying him of the board meeting had called him back to work.

It amazed him that Meg had never asked him to stay longer. Taylor had done everything in her power to keep him by her side, keep her financial security close. But Meg had only asked him to stay and provide her town with a medical service. And he'd grown to love Laurelton and the people. He'd make sure he visited, and not just during the snow season.

He tucked some stray hair from her face, his fingers caressing her temple. 'You know I have to go back.'

She stiffened for a moment. 'We never planned for more than this.'

'No.' The word hung between them. But what else was there to say? *What about 'Come with me'?*

A piece of firewood popped loudly in the silence.

Meg spoke softly. 'You're saving kids in your way, I'm saving the farm. We would never have even given each other a second glance if the plane hadn't crashed. This is the way it's meant to be.'

A sense of unease ran through him at her words. Was it the way it was meant to be? A brief interlude in their lives?

The conviction he'd always had about leaving suddenly started to tremble on shaky ground.

His phone vibrated, displaying the company secretary's number. Damn.

His life had been reduced to triage—difficult choices, limited outcomes and a hell of a lot of pain.

CHAPTER TEN

EXTREME fatigue clung to Meg like a blanket. Every action she took felt like wading through mud. And sleep, what was that? She'd spent fourteen nights tossing and turning, missing Will's arms and legs wrapped around her, missing the soothing sound of his regular breathing, missing him completely.

Nausea rolled through her. Tonight she must sleep. She couldn't function much more like this, and as much as she wanted to curl up, too many people depended on her. Laurelton needed her, her mother needed her and the farm needed more than she knew how to give.

She sighed and parked her car in the visitors' car park at the Winston rehabilitation unit. Eleanor had moved from the ward to Rehab a few days ago to focus on her physiotherapy, with the aim of coming home.

With a start, Meg remembered she must make an appointment with the occupational therapist to arrange for rails and bars to be installed in her mother's bathroom. She jotted the note in her diary among the mass of different coloured sticky notes. Reminders that threatened to swamp her. Again the urge to curl up and ignore everything pulled hard.

Bright, cheery curtains fluttered in the spring breeze as she walked along the corridor to Eleanor's room, clutching flowers, clean clothes and the manila folder that held the fate of the farm. Why had her mother let things get to this point?

Her mother sat by the window, dressed in a tracksuit and cross-stitching a sampler. The sunshine highlighted the black rings under her eyes.

With a jolt, Meg realised her mother was getting old. 'Hi, Mum.' Meg walked over and kissed Eleanor's cheek. 'Have they been working you hard?'

Eleanor smiled, looking very tired. 'Those physios make drill sergeants look like softies.'

Meg laughed and turned toward the sink, her back to her mother. She filled the vase with water. 'The sooner you get full range of movement, the sooner you'll be home.'

Her mother didn't respond.

Meg swivelled around to find Eleanor had dropped her cross stitch onto her lap and was staring out the window. 'Penny for them?'

A sigh shuddered through Eleanor's body. 'I don't know if the farm is home anymore, Meg.'

A cold sensation ran through her as she put the vase on the table. 'Of course it's home. You and Dad raised a family there, loved each other, it's part of you both.' *It's part of me.*

Her mother met her gaze, worry and exhaustion lines evident on her face. 'Since your dad died my life's been a series of battles. I've battled grief and I'm battling MS, as well as the bank. And as much as I love you dearly, and I know you love the farm, I just can't do it anymore.' She took in a deep breath. 'I'm sorry, but I'm going to sell the farm.'

No! Meg squatted by her mother's side, trying to ignore the dizziness that whizzed in her head.

'I can help more. I can look at renegotiating the loan, and I can—'

Her mother placed her hand on Meg's hair. 'It isn't just the struggle to meet the mortgage. I'm tired, Meg. I've worked hard all my life and now I want to be in town, close to my friends, and enjoy what useful time I have left.'

How could she argue with that? Her mother had a right to live her life her way. But she couldn't let the farm be sold. 'I've got a good job. I'll buy it from you.'

Pity crossed her mother's face. 'Meg, sometimes we have to let go.'

Meg's voice rose hysterically. 'I don't want to let go. It's all I've got.' Dread surfed through her, mixing with the nausea. Her head pounded, and her mother's face started to blur. Then blackness rolled in.

Meg squinted against a bright light above her.

A brisk voice spoke. 'Good. You're awake. You're in Winston Accident and Emergency because you fainted, bumped your head and had a short LOC.'

LOC? Loss of consciousness. She could remember talking to her mother about the farm but not much else.

'I'm Jenna, by the way.' The nurse gave her a reassuring smile. 'I think we've met before, at a meeting?'

'Meg Watson. Community Health Nurse at Laurelton.' She tried to move, her hands finding the cot sides on the edge of the narrow trolley.

'Just a mo, we'll sit you up.' The nurse fiddled behind her and with a clunk of metal on metal the top part of the trolley rose. 'Better?'

'Yes, thanks.' Confusion made Meg's brain foggy. 'Why did I faint?'

'That's what we're going to find out. You don't have a fever but your blood pressure's a bit low. We'll take some blood but a urine sample would be good. Do you think you can oblige?' The nurse produced a bedpan.

'Surely I can walk to the bathroom?' She didn't fancy balancing precariously on the green plastic.

Jenna laughed. 'Nurses and doctors make the worst patients. Sorry, but you're not walking anywhere for another hour.' She handed Meg the buzzer then tugged the curtains of the cubicle closed.

Meg thought of the Laurelton River racing across its smooth bed of stones and managed to comply with the request.

Jenna arrived almost immediately after the buzzer sounded. 'I'll test it for protein, glucose, ketones, all the usual stuff. Back in a jiff.'

Meg sat up even further, testing her head. The spinning sensation thankfully didn't return. Exhaustion was probably the culprit. Hopefully she'd be out of here quickly because she had to get to the head office of the bank in Melbourne and discuss ways to finance her purchase of the farm.

She wished she had a pad and pencil to write down everything she needed to do. Was her business suit dry-cleaned and ready for an outing? If she was going to be taken seriously by the bank, she had to have serious clothes.

Jenna returned, holding Meg's history, and closed the curtains behind her. 'I've got good news.'

Meg relaxed. 'Great. I doubted I had diabetes

as there's no family history and I hadn't been excessively thirsty. I'm sure I'm just overtired.'

Jenna smiled. 'Actually, you're pregnant. Congratulations!'

Meg heard the words but couldn't comprehend them. 'Sorry?'

'You're pregnant.' Jenna showed her the pregnancy test.

Meg's eyes struggled to focus on the plus sign in the middle of the test kit. 'But I can't be pregnant. We used condoms.'

'Condoms are ninety-five per cent effective, your baby is the five per cent failure rate.' Jenna looked serious for a moment. 'Are you OK?'

Meg nodded, 'I'm OK, just a bit shocked, but good shocked if you know what I mean.' Confusion swirled inside her. 'The thing is, I've got badly scarred tubes and my gynaecologist told me pregnancy was impossible.'

Jenna giggled. 'Don't you love proving those doctors wrong? Talking about doctors, you'll have to see Dr Sharman before you can be discharged, but I'd say you fainted because of low blood pressure caused by the pregnancy.' She jotted something down on the clipboard in her hand. 'Oh, and you should see your gynaecologist or, should I say, obstetrician.' She sighed. 'I just love pregnancies.' Placing her hand on Meg's arm, she gave her a reassuring squeeze. 'Take it easy and get some rest.'

Meg watched Jenna leave in a haze of disbelief. Her mind raced, unable to fix on any one thought. Pregnant. Her heart sang at the longed-for dream that had suddenly become a reality.

She was going to be a mother.

Will would be a father. A wonderful father.

Will.

She had to tell him. He'd be shocked, like her, but surely this was a good shock. Would he be as thrilled as she was? Did he want to be a father?

A kernel of fear twisted inside her. He might not want this. But, no matter what, he had to know.

This sort of news wasn't something she could do over the phone—it needed to be done in person.

Her planned day in Melbourne suddenly looked full—a visit to the gynaecologist, followed by an appointment at the bank. She'd save the best visit for last. Will.

Will's attention wandered from the column of figures in front of him and he gazed out at the tall black skyscraper that dominated the outlook from his building. He'd only just got back to the office, having been out all morning at the Royal Children's Hospital.

After his meeting he'd dropped in on Josh. He'd needed a 'patient fix' after missing the one-on-one contact he'd had in Laurelton. It had been great to spend time with the courageous little boy.

But during the visit he'd had half an ear listening for Meg. Hoping she would walk in, put her hands on his shoulders and lean in close, her laughing voice whispering in his ear, announcing her arrival.

But that was wishful thinking. Meg was in Laurelton.

And he'd been back in Melbourne a couple of weeks. Well, his body was back in Melbourne but his head was firmly in the country with Meg. She filled his thoughts, filled his dreams and when faced with a tricky issue he found himself wondering what her opinion would be.

In the past he'd never had any problem walking away from a woman. This time it was proving impossible.

He'd lost count of the number of occasions he'd picked up the phone to ring her, only to put it down again. What was he going to say? 'How's the weather? Are the alpine spring flowers out yet? Do you miss me as much as I miss you, so much that it hurts?'

No, it would be better to go and visit her.

He flicked his diary open, looking for a free weekend when he could get down to see her.

His intercom buzzed and his secretary's voice sounded down the line. 'Will, are you free to see a Ms Watson? She doesn't have an appointment.'

Meg. He jumped to his feet and hauled open the office door, his heart beating fast, his arms aching to hold her.

'Meg.'

She swivelled around on a pair of fine stiletto heels looking—looking like a city version of his country girl. She'd swept back her hair into a knot at the base of her neck, straightening out every curl, although he noticed one had thankfully escaped, softening the prim look.

From the fine wool skirt to the fitted jacket and the gold chain around her neck, she looked every inch like the women he'd always avoided. Designer-clad, corporate sharks, determined to land their fish. For the first time he saw a flash of Taylor.

He shook his head. Meg was nothing like Taylor.

But right now she didn't look anything like his Meg either.

He found his voice, which had stalled at the sight of her. 'Come in. It's lovely to see you.'

She smiled a nervous smile and walked ahead of him into the office.

He closed the door and reached for her.

She came into his arms, her scent of wild flowers tantalising him. He immediately released the clasp on her hair, pulling it free, letting her hair cascade down her back, the curls exploding from their straitjacket.

He plunged his face into her hair and breathed deep. 'That's better.'

She gave a tight smile. 'Didn't you like my city hair?'

'You don't need city hair, you're a country girl.' He kissed her, revelling in her taste of sweet sunshine and freshly mown hay.

He brought his head up and gazed into her blue eyes. 'It's so good to see you. I've missed you.'

She caressed his cheek with her fingers. 'I've missed you, too.'

'I was just planning a visit to you.' He wrapped a curl around his finger, feeling like a kid who had just discovered a stash of hidden sweets.

She leaned in close and put her hands on his shoulders. Rising up on her toes, she spoke close to his ear, her voice low. 'I beat you to it.'

Desire thudded through him, driving every rational thought from his head. God, he wanted her. Wanted to bury himself inside her and forget everything that wasn't working in his life.

She stepped back out of his arms, her initial nervousness returning. 'Can I have a drink of water, please?'

He started. 'Of course.' He poured a glass of iced water from a jug and handed it to her, noticing shadows around her eyes that hadn't been there when he'd last seen her.

She downed the water in two gulps.

'How's Eleanor?' He refilled the glass.

'She's in Rehab.'

An unfamiliar air of anxiety hovered about her and he wanted to banish it. He sat down in an easy chair and pulled her down onto his lap, her legs across his body. 'Sit down. I can't imagine those heels are very comfortable. Why are you dressed like this?'

Wariness washed over her face. 'I had two important meetings today—well, three really.'

He pulled off her shoes and ran his hand along the top of her foot and up her stockinged leg, 'Hopefully one was with the Health Department. I suggested to the Minister that Laurelton needed a service review.'

'Uh, no, it wasn't with the department.' Her voice sounded disconcerted. She put her hand over his, stalling it at mid-thigh. 'Um, there's no easy way to say this. I saw my gynaecologist today.'

A thread of unease stirred inside him. 'Why?'
'I'm pregnant.'

His breath stalled in his chest as her words boomed in his head. Disbelief roared in his ears and he struggled to think. Condoms, they'd used condoms.

They don't always work. The voices of his family planning lecturers played across his mind. Pregnant. A child.

His child.

His and Meg's child.

A seed of happiness and pure joy expanded inside him. He tried to form the words to respond, but his mouth felt like it was full of cotton wool. This baby was a miracle for both of them. He wanted to hug her, sing, but he could only stare at her in glorious amazement.

Her eyes, bright blue with the wonder of the baby, stared at him as his silence extended. 'I...I know it's a shock.'

He managed to croak out the words, 'It's a wonderful shock, the best kind.'

She hugged him hard. 'I've had a week of shocks. Straight after the appointment with my doctor I had a meeting at the bank's head office.' She bit her lip. 'After all of Mum's and my hard work, Big Hill Farm has to be sold unless I can find the three hundred and fifty thousand dollars to re-establish the loan.'

Her voice caught and tears filmed her eyes. 'I can't believe I'm going to lose one hundred and fifty years of my family's heritage.'

Three hundred and fifty thousand dollars. He stiffened and dropped his hand from her thigh, almost pushing her off his lap. Money. She needed money. *His* money. Her words replayed in his head. *I think I'd do just about anything to keep the farm.*

His chest tightened. She was no different from all the other women he'd ever met. She'd use him to get what she needed. She was the same as Taylor.

Ignoring the stunned look on her face as she stumbled to her feet, he let his anger blast through him in righteous fury. 'So you need a loan?'

She flinched at his tone. 'I do, but—'

'And this baby is the collateral, is it?

'What?' Her face paled to white-on-white, confusion skating all over it.

'You told me it was impossible for you to conceive.'

Disbelief filled her eyes. 'I didn't lie to you. I'd been told I had scarring and blocked tubes and was unlikely to conceive.'

'And yet you're conveniently pregnant with my child, just as you need a truckload of money to save your precious farm. What a coincidence.'

Her gasp echoed around the room. 'What are you really saying?'

'You know what I'm saying. You get pregnant, I marry you and *my* money saves your farm. All very neat, isn't it?'

She gripped the back of a chair, her knuckles white as understanding dawned on her face. 'You think I set you up?' Incredulity clung to her words. 'This pregnancy is a million-to-one chance, and you know it.'

His jaw ached from rigid tension. 'I think you're using this baby to get what you want.'

'I don't think you're thinking at all.' She wrung her hands and her body trembled.

He blocked her actions out, his anger not wanting to acknowledge her shock. 'I've had women try to marry me in the past, but none of them have stooped so low as to involve an innocent child.'

Her cheeks blazed pink, as if she'd been slapped. 'You spent three weeks with me yet you have no idea who I am.'

Her whispered words sliced into him. For a brief moment he hesitated in his conviction about her. But years of conditioning thundered in, flattening the fledgling thought. *Women only want you for your money. None of them love you.*

He grabbed a cheque-book and with a shaking hand filled in the blanks. 'I'll provide for my child and my lawyer will be in touch with you to arrange access and maintenance. This will cover what you need for the pregnancy.' He ripped the cheque from the stub and held it out toward her, almost waving it under her nose. 'You came here for money so here it is.'

She stood her ground, tilting her head slightly to prevent the cheque from touching her. She spoke softly yet the words cut with jagged edges. 'I came here to tell you about the baby because, as the father, you have the right to know that your child will be coming into the world next year. I didn't come here begging for money.'

'Yeah, right.'

'Yeah, absolutely right.' She snatched the cheque and slammed it down onto his desk. 'I don't want your money. This child deserves to be free of the Cameron wealth. It sure as hell hasn't made you happy. For all your talk of not loving money, it's fast looking like the wheeling and dealing of the business world has you well and truly in its grip.'

The words slapped him. 'You don't know what you're talking about.'

Her eyes blazed at him, the dark blue of a summer storm. 'I know enough. You just accused me of forcing you into a marriage to get your money. I'm not the one forcing you to do anything. Has it occurred to you that perhaps your family are so thrilled that you're working in the business that maybe they're not trying that hard to find a replacement? Or that your dad is not coming back to work as fast as he possibly could because he's so happy to have you alongside him, doing the job he never thought you would do?'

Unease washed through him, making him defensive. 'That's just plain crazy. He's been bloody sick.'

She crossed her arms, standing firm. 'Do you think in their love for you their intentions might be misguided, that they're trying to have a repeat performance of their life in you? Have the heir run the company?' Understanding edged across her face. 'You once told me that your parents' marriage was traditional, a business merger, that their job was to run Camerons and produce an heir, didn't you?'

He didn't want to hear this, he wanted the words to stop. 'And you're stepping up to the plate to provide the next heir, aren't you?' The words sounded harsh, leaving the taste of regret in his mouth.

Her jaw clenched. 'This isn't about me, it's all about you.' She stepped toward him, putting her hand on his sleeve. Empathy stirred in her eyes. 'Why are you letting this situation at Camerons slide on with no end in sight? You've done your part, paid your dues, been a caring and loving son.'

Her warmth seeped into him, trying to soothe. He threw off her hand, hating the betrayal of his body to her touch. Hating how close to the truth she was. 'You don't have any idea of what you're talking about.'

'I think I do. You've enjoyed this time, getting to know your father. You've had a chance you missed out on as a kid, and you made him a promise you don't want to break. But it isn't making you happy.'

Self-righteous honour filled him. 'I have a duty to my father and by running KKC I am saving kids' lives. As a nurse, you surely understand that.'

Her logical gaze pierced him. 'I do, but you're not doing it in the best way.'

He hated her unrelenting stare and resorted to sarcasm. 'And you'd know what the best way is, would you?'

She nodded. 'I've got a better idea than you. Right now you're living your father's dream, not yours. You know you can't look me straight in the eye and tell me you're happy.'

He folded his arms. 'Being happy isn't necessarily life's goal.'

Her face showed signs of exasperation mingled with sympathy. 'You're right—but your skills as a doctor make you happy and they help so many people. You have a gift as a doctor and you're throwing it away. Talk to your father, tell him how you really feel, tell him what you want to do. Reclaim your life.'

Her words bombarded him and he hated the clarity she seemed to have on his situation, which he'd not been able to see. 'My life is my own now.'

'You're deluding yourself if you really believe that.' She wrapped her arms around her body. 'A few weeks ago I fell in love with a wonderful, generous and caring man. But today I've seen exactly what this wealth and a misguided sense of duty are really doing to you. It's making you bitter and miserable.'

Bile scalded his throat. 'If I'm bitter, it's to do with your betrayal.'

Her eyes flashed for a moment and then the spark faded. She took in a long, slow breath. 'I didn't betray you, Will. I loved you. This child is a miracle, conceived in love. But you can't recognise that. You once said money gets in the way of love. That only happens if you let it.'

She walked toward the door, pausing as she turned the handle. 'You're using money to do great things and yet you're letting it poison you. Goodbye, Will.'

Her quietly spoken words punched him hard as the door clicked shut behind her.

He kicked his rubbish bin hard, his frustration overflowing. What did she really know about his life, about his complicated role in a family dynasty, about his relationship with his father?

He picked up the bin, scooping the balls of paper back into it. *Right now you're living your father's dream, not yours.* The silence in the room bore down on him, heavy with the significance of her words.

His anger fizzled.

In ten minutes Meg, with a few well-chosen words, had reduced his life to the bare bones. How had he missed what was really important to him?

His father's illness had scared him and he'd made a promise generated by love and fear. And, sure, the business side of things hadn't done a thing for him, but KKC and the new relationship with his father had energised him.

But Meg was right. He desperately missed medicine, the kids and their parents who made his day. Working in Laurelton had rammed that home loud and clear. When he was practising medicine he was whole.

As each month had passed and his father's physical frailness had continued, he'd turned more and more to KKC for work satisfaction. He'd convinced himself it was working, that KKC made up for the medicine he missed, that he could do more for patients by providing vital research funds. He was involved in every facet of the submission and allocation process, he was actively building the trust, he was…damn miserable.

Meg was right. He had to talk to his father, had to force the issue of a replacement. His cousin would be perfect for the job—after all, he had more business acumen in his little finger than Will had in his whole body. He had to risk the closeness he had with his father because his own unhappiness might tarnish it in the future.

Suddenly it all seemed so clear and simple.

Why hadn't he been able to see if before? Meg had worked it out way ahead of him.

Meg.

He raised his eyes to the closed door. What had he just done? He sat down hard on his desk chair and ran his hands though his hair. In his fury he'd just driven away the only woman he had ever loved.

The only woman he had ever loved.

The realisation stunned him, and he struggled to breathe.

He loved her.

He swivelled around and stared out the window. What a fool he'd been. He must have loved her for weeks, but he'd been so wrapped up in his own baggage that he'd missed the best thing that had ever happened to him. He thumped his desk with his fist, welcoming the dull ache that radiated up his arm.

And just to stuff things up completely, he'd let his past relationships slither in and dominate his thinking. How had he let that happen?

He stood up and poured himself a large mug of coffee. It had been her unexpected arrival, the different clothes, her unusual hesitancy, combined with the news of the baby and the farm that had completely disarmed him. He'd let Taylor's legacy march in and take control.

God, he was a fool. Of all the things he could accuse Meg of, being a gold-digger wasn't one of them. She was forthright, independent, organised but generous to a fault. She'd never asked him for anything except to be a doctor to Laurelton. Hell, she hadn't even charged him board at Big Hill Farm.

And yet he'd stupidly forgotten all that and had let fly with hurtful words, driving her and his baby out of his life.

He'd been so wrong. The bitter taste of over-brewed coffee scalded his throat, but he didn't care.

He'd sworn off relationships after Taylor. Yet it had only taken one woman with riotous hair the colour of sun-kissed barley to turn his life upside down and open his eyes to what was really important.

He picked up the phone. He'd put his professional life in order, talk to his dad and then he'd go and see Meg.

If he had to beg for forgiveness, he'd do it. This time he wasn't going to let the best thing in his life walk away from him.

She'd given him one hell of a wake-up call.

He hoped with every fibre of his being she'd still want him in her life.

CHAPTER ELEVEN

MEG stood on the veranda, staring out across the home paddock, immune to the bright yellow daffodils that usually made her feel full of enthusiasm for the warmer days of spring. Instead, her gaze was riveted on the FOR SALE sign that had recently been nailed to the fence.

In the past four days she'd exhausted every avenue she knew of to generate funds to save the farm. Her brothers were ambivalent, having disengaged from it long ago.

Grief swirled with happiness, making a strange sensation in the pit of her stomach. The news of her pregnancy still had her awestruck. Unbelievably, just as her dream of a baby was being realised, her dream of raising her child on the farm was being dashed against the dirt.

Her child.

She would be raising this child alone.

One last dream trampled—the one where she shared the raising of her family alongside a loving partner.

Sharp pain slashed at her and she bit her lip to stop the tears that hovered, now so much a part of her since she'd left Will's office. For days she'd relived their conversation over and over and over, still shocked that he believed she'd deliberately got pregnant to save the farm. That everything they'd shared had been part of some grand plan devised by her to use him.

She hadn't been so naïve and stupid as to think Will wouldn't be shocked or surprised about the pregnancy. But she also knew she'd fallen in love with a man who had so many wonderful qualities that she'd assumed, after the initial stunned reaction, he'd be just as excited about the baby as she was.

Never in her wildest dreams had she imagined he'd accuse her of gold-digging.

She spun around, turning her back on the depressing sign, and walked into the house, returning to packing boxes. She quickly folded a box, creating it from flat cardboard, and started loading it with books. Slowly stacking away her childhood memories, stories she'd read by torch-light under the covers after her dad had kissed her goodnight. Jet ambled in and sat down, watching her with doleful eyes.

She wiped her own eyes and breathed in a shuddering breath. Life was tough. As a farmer's daughter, she'd never doubted it. But some things were tougher than others. Packing up her childhood memories into a box was a stark reminder of all she was losing. But it paled compared to a life without Will.

'So, that's it for this week.' Meg pasted a smile on her face as her diabetic education group came to a close. She loved her job but the fatigue of early pregnancy was taking its toll. The group were in-credibly supportive of each other and Meg left them chatting in the meeting room, knowing that her health-education talks were just one small part of why ten people gathered together each month. Most of the value of the group came from people coming together to share experiences.

Letting her mind go into neutral, she filed away the patient histories and her gaze drifted to the clock. She had another hour to go before she could head home to an exciting night of even more packing.

A soft knock on her opened door made her turn.

Will stood tall, filling the doorway. New lines were etched deeply around his eyes, but apart from that little else looked different. His jeans hugged his long legs and his long-sleeved striped polo shirt picked up the green in his eyes. Casual yet deadly.

Her heart skipped a beat, thrilled to see him. Then reality hit her. He was probably only here to formalise arrangements regarding the baby. She slammed the filing cabinet shut. The clashing sound filled the air between them.

'May I come in?'

His excessively polite tone ripped at her, reinforcing the loss of their previous shared joyfulness at seeing each other.

'Take a seat.' She gestured to a chair opposite her and sat down behind the desk, needing the barrier between them.

He put his hand on the back of the chair, as if

he was going to move it to the side of the desk, but after a slight hesitation he left it where it was and sat down.

'Meg, I—'

'Meg!'

A frantic voice and running feet propelled Meg quickly out of her chair. She heard the scraping of Will's chair against the floorboards and knew he was following her.

She almost ran into Jenny D'Angelo, who was cuddling Sarah, her two-year-old daughter. 'What's wrong, Jenny?'

'Sarah was having her afternoon nap and I went in to wake her up and she isn't right. She's agitated and restless and it's not just the normal being slow to wake up.' Her voice trembled. 'I'm really worried.'

'We need to examine her.' Will stepped forward and ushered the terrified woman into the treatment room.

Meg grabbed a stethoscope, passing it to Will before she unwrapped the very pale child from her blanket. The nose-tingling odour of camphor rose strongly from the blanket.

'Jenny, have you been using camphor rub on Sarah?' Meg swivelled around so she could see the woman's face.

The worried mother nodded. 'She's had a cold and I've been putting it on her chest.'

'Is there any way she could have got to the container?'

Jenny's eyes reflected her frazzled state as she tried to think. 'I rubbed her chest and then she asked for her bottle and I put the container down and… Oh, God, I left it in the cot.'

Meg met Will's gaze for a moment, the unspoken thought of poisoning almost palpable between them. Each time it happened she was amazed at how in sync they were professionally. Her heart bled that it couldn't be transferred into their personal life.

'I'll check her mouth.' Will examined Sarah's mouth for signs of the camphor rub. If Sarah had ingested it, she was one desperately sick little girl.

Quickly, Meg pulled the child's clothing off her.

Sarah started to sob and then vomited. Sobs turned into screams as the camphor burned her oesophagus.

'Sorry, sweetie, but we need to take your clothes off. Mummy's here.' Meg tilted her head, inviting Jenny to come over and comfort Sarah. 'We have to wash her, Jenny, and get all the rub off her skin as soon as possible.'

The desperate mother just stood and stared.

'Jenny, how much does Sarah weigh?' Will's calm and quiet voice seemed to focus Jenny.

'She's twelve kilograms. Why?'

Deep lines marked Will's face. 'We're pretty certain Sarah has camphor poisoning. We're going to give her activated charcoal to absorb the camphor and the dose is based on weight.'

'It's dangerous?' The woman shook her head, as if trying to understand what was going on around her.

'It's extremely toxic when it's eaten.'

The flat tone in his voice panicked Meg. She knew he was extremely worried and he didn't worry unduly.

He rubbed the back of his neck. 'Jenny, have you noticed any muscle twitching on Sarah's body?'

'No.' Hysteria encased the word.

Meg quickly passed a bowl of water and washcloths to Jenny. 'You need to wash her, using a lot of soap and water.' She put her hand on the woman's arm. 'I know you're scared, but I need your help while I help Will.'

Jenny swallowed a sob and started to wash Sarah.

'I'll get the charcoal.' She crossed the room and opened the drawer, her eyes scanning the containers.

'Meg, she's fitting. Get diazepam.' Will grabbed an airway and inserted it into Sarah's throat.

Jenny's gasping cry echoed around the room.

'Butterfly needle or IV cannula?' Meg gave him both as she quickly put a tourniquet around the little girl's arm.

'Swap you. You hold her and I'll put in the drip.' Will waited until Meg had her hand on Sarah before stepping away.

Her mind fired out a list of instructions— control airway before administering charcoal.

The toddler's body shuddered and Meg marvelled at how Will managed to insert the IV needle and administer the drug. Almost like magic, the diazepam worked and the muscle spasms faded. Sarah lay still but unconscious.

'Will she be all right?'

Jenny's fear-laden question lanced Meg and she glanced at Will's tight face, wanting the same reassurance as Jenny. Knowing it wasn't going to be on offer.

Will's mouth firmed into a straight line. 'We're doing all we can but Sarah will have to be airlifted out. She needs to be in ICU. I'm sorry, Jenny, but I need Meg's help here. You must ring the ambulance and relay my words down the phone line. Use the phone on the wall over there.' Will tilted his head toward the white handset.

For a moment Jenny was silent, but then she straightened as if she'd found a reserve of strength. 'Of course, Doctor. I'll do it now.'

Meg stroked Sarah's blonde hair while she spoke. 'You're going to have to intubate her before we give the charcoal, aren't you?'

Will grimaced and nodded. 'We need to control her airway. Her respiratory centre is being depressed by the camphor.'

She bit her lip. 'She's lucky you're here.'

His eyes darkened for a moment. 'I didn't come here for Sarah.'

Hope surged inside her, rolling through every part of her until it crashed into reason. Will wasn't there for her either.

'Once we've tubed her, we'll insert a nasogastric tube and give her the charcoal.'

His words brought Meg's mind back to task. 'Right, I'll get the equipment.'

'Doctor, I've got the operator on the line.' Jenny held out the phone.

'Tell them that Sarah has camphor poisoning, she's being intubated and we require paediatric emergency evacuation.'

Jenny turned back to the call and repeated the message.

The laryngoscope felt cold and heavy in Meg's hand as she passed it to Will.

Carefully, he inserted the small silver instrument into Sarah's little mouth. Lines of concentration like trenches deepened on his brow. 'I can see the vocal cords.' He put his hand out for the tube.

Meg silently placed the tube into his hand and waited with a syringe in the other, ready to inflate the balloon that would hold the tube in place.

'Gotcha. I'm in.' He turned and grinned at Meg, relief written all over his face.

Her knees wobbled. She knew the smile had nothing to do with her but she'd take it anyway. It was probably the last smile of his she'd be party to. His prejudice about her would see to that.

'I'll bag her and you insert the nasogastric tube—unless you want me to?' His clear gaze held hers.

The tear in her heart ripped wide open and gaped. Professionally he was always so considerate, a real team player. In the past she'd treasured that. Today it amplified all she'd lost.

'I'll do it.' Her words shot out briskly, trying to give the impression she was in control when really control hung by a thread. She snapped on a pair of gloves, measured the distance from Sarah's nose to the right angle of her jaw and then the approximate length to her stomach. Meg gently inserted the narrow plastic tube into Sarah's left nostril, guiding it down the oesophagus.

It felt good to have something concrete to focus on. She clicked a syringe to the end of the tube and pulled back, checking for stomach contents.

Will handed her a stethoscope, pre-empting

her next step of checking that the tube was in the correct position. Sarah didn't need activated charcoal in her lungs and occasionally the tube went into the trachea instead of the stomach.

Injecting air into the tube, Meg listened for the *glur-glub* sound in Sarah's stomach. 'It's in the right place.' She whipped the stethoscope out of her ears and quickly taped the tube into position.

'Swap you back while you administer the charcoal.' A swoop of heat whizzed through her as their hands brushed on the change-over.

'Doctor?' Jenny clutched a notepad. 'The paediatric team need you to ring them on their mobile and the helicopter is set to arrive in forty minutes.'

'Thanks, Jenny. I'm sorry you had to do that but we've got Sarah stable for the moment.' He seemed to swallow a sigh. 'I'm giving her the charcoal now and we'll monitor her vital signs closely. We've had to put a tube into her throat to keep her airway open and a drip so we can give drugs to prevent any more seizures.'

Jenny tentatively approached the examination table where Sarah lay white and still. Her hand flew to her mouth and she stifled a sob before reaching out and holding her child's hand.

'Once she's in ICU in Melbourne, I'll be a lot happier. She's a very sick little girl.' For the umpteenth time, Will rubbed the back of his neck.

They all fell silent, waiting for the sound of the helicopter, willing it to arrive. All words seemed inadequate.

For the second time in weeks, Meg found herself in the Laurelton pub's car park, walking away from the emergency helicopter with Will by her side. This time his pensive mood pervaded her, dragging at her, heightening her misery.

As she turned toward the clinic his hand caught her arm. 'Could we go and sit in the park for a bit?'

She sighed. Did it really matter where their relationship officially ended? 'OK.' She stepped away from his hand, needing the space, determined to avoid the contact, knowing his touch would completely undermine her determination to stay detached.

The tulips' bright and cheery heads stood tall, turning the park from winter browns into a vibrant rainbow of colour. A wooden park bench with a decorative back sat nestled between two large magnolia trees. The perfume from the large flowers wafted past on the gentle breeze.

Normally the park made her heart sing. Today it was the antithesis of her feelings. She sat on the far end of the bench.

Will sat at the other end, leaning forward and lacing his fingers as his hands rested between his knees. His gaze appeared to pass the fountain in the middle of the park and look out toward the mountain range, the jagged peak of Mt Hume being the highest point. He sighed, a long shuddering breath.

Finally he moved around and stared at her, the brown and green of his eyes swirling with a myriad of emotions. He spoke quietly in the same serious tone he'd used with Jenny. 'Meg, there's a few things we need to work out.'

Her jaw stiffened. So this was it. This was the businessman's son reducing their child to a commodity, the one thing he'd once said a child should never be. 'I'm surprised you didn't send a Cameron Enterprises lawyer.'

Confusion washed over his face and then understanding dawned. 'I said my lawyer would be in touch, didn't I?' He ran his hand through his hair. 'I also said a lot of other unforgivable things.'

The supplication in his voice tore at her. 'You did.' She forced herself to stay aloof. She had to stay strong for the baby.

'Hell, Meg, if I could take back those words I hurled at you, I would.' He reached for her hand. 'I'm so incredibly sorry.'

She stiffened, letting her hand rest impassively in his, trying to disconnect from his touch.

'I've spent years avoiding women, and you walked into my life with your enthusiasm, your convictions, and you didn't want anything from me. I'd never experienced that before, couldn't believe it was possible.'

He swallowed hard. 'You're the most amazing woman I've ever met and I let my past ruin the best thing that has ever happened to me. I wanted to run after you almost as soon as you left and ask you to forgive me, but I knew I had to make some changes in my life first.'

His thumb caressed her hand in delicate circles, sending showers of delicious longing cascading through her. *He'd wanted to run after her.* Her heart skipped but common sense sent it back into its normal rhythm.

With superhuman effort she concentrated on his words. 'What changes?'

'You rightfully levelled some home truths at me. Working down here with you, I realised how much I missed hands-on medicine. But I was torn. Working beside my father had given me a closeness with him that I'd never had and his illness scared me. What if this time was the only time I had with him? So I let it drag on, convincing myself that KKC was still medicine. I lost my sense of purpose.'

He smiled at her. 'It took you to point that out. I'm going back to finish paediatrics.'

Surprise followed by joy for him tumbled through her. She squeezed his hand. 'That's wonderful. I'm really pleased for you. It's where you belong.'

She tried to hold off the sadness that slid instantly over the joy. He was organising his life.

Getting back on track. A separate life from her and the baby.

'How did your dad react to the news?'

'He thanked me for stepping in and avoiding Camerons being taken over by a rival company and giving him the help when he needed it. He told me he loved me very much but I'd never make a businessman.' Will laughed. 'He was waiting for me to say I'd had enough and I was waiting for him to step back in.' His fingertips stroked the back of her hand with a feather-like touch.

She tried to steel herself against the flood of sensation that swept through her body.

Will continued. 'He's accepted my suggestion that my cousin, Anthony, is the future for Camerons.' His intent gaze scanned her face. 'You were right, we needed to talk. How did you get to be so wise?'

She pulled her hand away from his. She couldn't do this much longer. 'Will, I'm really pleased you've sorted out your life and got back on track. But I can't be your life coach. You started this con-versation with "We've got a few things to sort out", and we do. Between us we have a child and—'

'Meg, I love you.'

The words thudded into her, turning her breath solid in her chest. 'What?'

'Hell, I'm stuffing this up, too.' He moved toward her and gathered her close. 'I love you. I love our child that is growing inside you and I love the idea that we're a family.'

Her heart hammered while her brain tried to absorb the news. She put her hand up and touched his face. 'I've loved you since you held me and kept me warm in a snow cave on Mt Hume.'

He squeezed her against him. 'You give me what I need. You're my friend, my lover and my guide. I want to be with you every day of my life.' Sorrow filled his eyes. 'But I can't be in Laurelton and I can't ask you to leave here.'

'Why not?' She'd come this far, she wasn't going to lose him now.

'Because you belong in Laurelton, your family's heritage is here, your mother is here and so is your job.'

Her heart sang at his love and consideration for her. 'Three months ago I would have thought the same thing. I've been hiding behind the farm and, as you pointed out, it wasn't a viable dream. This last week has shown me that life without you isn't life at all.'

He kissed her so hard stars exploded in her head.

She pulled back, laughing. 'Hey, don't deprive the baby of oxygen.'

He grinned, but just as quickly his face became serious. 'I have a plan I want to discuss with you. Do you remember I talked to the Minister about Laurelton's health-care needs?'

'Vaguely. More Cameron strings?' She raised her brows.

He looked sheepish. 'Call it networking. Anyway, based on current data, the growth of the region and of the township of Winston, there is a need for a paediatrician. I have to do one more year in Melbourne but after that you, the baby and I can live in Winston and be close to your mother. This baby can have a country upbringing. I know it's not Laurelton but it's the country and—'

She threw her arms around his neck, hugging him hard. She sat back, a thought coming to her. 'How does that work in with KKC?'

'We'll have to go to Melbourne for some fund-raising but we're going to get our local community involved down here. I envisage satellite groups all over the country working to raise funds. The true spirit of the country will drive KKC.'

He'd thought it all through, worked it all out. Guilt slithered through her. 'What about Laurelton? I can't just leave them without any health care at all.'

'You won't be. We'll sort it out. Your reliever might be interested in full-time work for a year until you're back in the region, and we'll also lobby for a GP. The type of medical scenarios we've had in the last few weeks gives plenty of ammunition to prove a case. I promise you, Laurelton will be looked after. I have a vested interest after all.'

'You do?' Surprise trickled through her.

'I do. My holiday house is here.' His eyes sparkled with mischief.

She didn't know whether to be happy or worried. 'What other changes have you made?'

He picked up both her hands. 'I know how devastated you are about losing the farm and I am so sorry that I ever said that you—'

She raised her finger to his lips. 'Shh, that's over.'

He kissed her hand. 'I've spoken to Eleanor and she's arranging for the house and the home paddock to be on a different title prior to sale. I can't give you the farm but I can give you the house.'

Stunned amazement washed over her. Big Hill Farm homestead, with all its memories and all its stories, was still part of her. Tears welled in her eyes and she had no power to stop them. She tried to speak but the words caught against the surge of love she had for this wonderful man.

'Meg, I want to grow old with you. Please, will you marry me in a field of silken daisies on the side of Mt Hume?'

She threw herself against him, feeling his hard chest against hers and his loving arms around her body. He loved her. He understood her and he wanted their child. 'Yes. A thousand times yes.'

EPILOGUE

BABY Thomas John Richard Cameron lay in his mother's arms replete, a belly full of nature's gold—breast milk. Meg cuddled him close as she rocked in the double rocker, back and forth, on the veranda of Big Hill homestead. Her gaze drifted from her son to the christening guests enjoying their afternoon tea on the lawn.

September sunshine shone over the party and Meg couldn't believe how blessed she was. She smiled down at little Tom as he snuffled in his milk-dream sleep and straightened the train of the christening gown. The Cameron christening gown.

Hilary, Will's mother, stepped up to the veranda, clutching two glasses of champagne in her hands. 'How's my grandson doing?'

Meg smiled at her mother-in-law, whose maternal instincts had finally surfaced with the arrival of her grandson. 'He's fine. Is that glass for me?'

'No, it's for your mother. She's good but she can't juggle crutches and a champagne flute.'

Meg laughed. Hilary had not only embraced her new daughter-in-law into the family, she'd also formed a close friendship with Eleanor. Hilary and Richard would often fly down to visit and stay at Big Hill Farm.

As Hilary wandered off, Will's father, Richard, sat down next to Meg. He ran his fingers over his grandson's downy head. 'So how old does this little one have to be before I can take him fishing?'

Meg smiled. Will and his dad often disappeared to fish. Their relationship, firmed by working together, hadn't faltered, as Will had feared. 'I think as soon as he can walk he'll want to be tagging along with his dad and his pa-pa.'

'Excellent. I can teach him to fish but Will can teach him to ski. I think my skiing days have finished.' He spied the food and stood up. 'I think I might just go and grab a plate of those tempting sandwiches. There's something about fresh air and country food.'

'It's good to see you with an appetite again.' Richard's health had continued to improve, much to everyone's delight.

Will slid into the rocker next to Meg, dropping his arm around her shoulder and stroking his son's cheek. 'Happy?'

She nodded and snuggled in close to him, welcoming the pressure of his leg against her own, his heat mixing with hers, marvelling at how her body responded to him every time he touched her. Glorying in the knowledge of how much she was loved.

'Having the christening here in my family's home, and having little Tom wearing your family's christening gown, well, it completes the circle, doesn't it?'

Love flared in his eyes. 'We're trailblazing new traditions. I don't expect my son to be a doctor or a businessman.'

She smiled. 'Or even a nurse or a farmer.'

His expression sobered. 'They say children take you to places you never expected to go.'

She stroked his cheek. 'True, but it will be a

journey we'll all take together. With you by my side I can't wait.'

He captured her lips in a kiss filled with promise. 'Neither can I.'

MEDICAL ROMANCE™

Large Print

Titles for the next three months...

June

THE MIDWIFE'S CHRISTMAS MIRACLE Sarah Morgan
ONE NIGHT TO WED Alison Roberts
A VERY SPECIAL PROPOSAL Josie Metcalfe
THE SURGEON'S MEANT-TO-BE BRIDE Amy Andrews
A FATHER BY CHRISTMAS Meredith Webber
A MOTHER FOR HIS BABY Leah Martyn

July

THE SURGEON'S MIRACLE BABY Carol Marinelli
A CONSULTANT CLAIMS HIS BRIDE Maggie Kingsley
THE WOMAN HE'S BEEN WAITING FOR
Jennifer Taylor
THE VILLAGE DOCTOR'S MARRIAGE Abigail Gordon
IN HER BOSS'S SPECIAL CARE Melanie Milburne
THE SURGEON'S COURAGEOUS BRIDE Lucy Clark

August

A WIFE AND CHILD TO CHERISH Caroline Anderson
THE SURGEON'S FAMILY MIRACLE Marion Lennox
A FAMILY TO COME HOME TO Josie Metcalfe
THE LONDON CONSULTANT'S RESCUE Joanna Neil
THE DOCTOR'S BABY SURPRISE Gill Sanderson
THE SPANISH DOCTOR'S CONVENIENT BRIDE
Meredith Webber

MILLS & BOON®

0507 LP 1P Medical

Roscommon County Library Service

WITHDRAWN FROM STOCK